SIGNS OF DECEPTION

Matthew J. Anderson

Copyright © 2021, Matthew J. Anderson

All rights reserved.

This book contains material protected under International and
Federal Copyright Laws and Treaties. Any unauthorized reprint
or use of this material is prohibited. No part of this book may
be reproduced or transmitted in any form or by any means,
electronic or mechanical, including photocopying, recording,
or by any information storage and retrieval system without
express written permission from the author / publisher.

A toast to my late aunt, Vicki Anderson, who inspired me to embrace my creativity and finish my first novel after a Coors Light cheers cling overlooking the glistening Gulf of Mexico at Crabby Bills on a beautiful spring day in St. Petersburg, Florida in March 2008.

CONTENTS

CHAPTER 1

"Come on. God damnit! You've got to make that fucking play!" Coach Edwards bellowed through his deep frightening tone while pacing down the sideline. He proceeded to kick over a large orange water cooler and let out a menacing roar. Delicious, refreshing Cool Blue Gatorade floated through the air and then in a split second gravity played grim reaper and brought the sports beverage to its demise into the ground. The entire football team gasped, flailing their hands in dismay knowing that was their last drop in the blistering ninety-two degrees heat. The rest of football practice was going to be a hell zone because thirst could no longer be cured for the next hour. At that daunting moment, Cool Blue resembled the elixir of life, but the potion and perhaps life itself had vanished into thin air.

Sweat dripped down from Coach Edward's hat brim and he hocked a loogie on the 50-yard line. Folding his arms, he let out a menacing roar—he just witnessed the "star athlete" drop a perfect pinpoint pass for a touchdown. With pleasure, he picked up his personal water bottle and took a very, long satisfying gulp glaring into the end-zone.

"Sorry, Coach, uh, um… the sun was in my eyes," Aaron said with a smirk using his hand to create a shield from the sun. The rest of the football team would have normally chuckled, but they were so disappointed with the Gatorade fiasco that they didn't have any interest to tune into Aaron's class clown shenanigans. Coach Edwards also wasn't amused and his face turned into a bright beaming red and raised his eyebrows in disgust. Coach Edwards wiped sweat off his face, scratched behind his head and slowly walked over to Aaron glaring into his eyes.

"Do you really think you can fuck with me?" Coach Edwards screamed. "I honestly can't take this shit anymore. If you guys don't want to win a damn state title, then fuck! Why am I here wasting my time trying to coach you arrogant pieces of shit? Go ahead and cheat your way through life if you want. You will fail. Always! It will not happen on my watch," he barked waving his hat and wiping sweat from his forehead from the blistering summer heat.

Coach Edwards was a muscular, tall, balding African American man accompanied by a temper that was known across the entire campus. He was a former Navy Seal sniper and there had been rumors that he preferred to assassinate the enemy by sneaking up on them rather than shooting them.

Teachers often complained about his weightlifting habits because his violent yet satisfying screams from using the bench press could be heard on the entire second floor. The principal ignored these concerns because he most likely didn't want to end up in a body bag himself. Edwards loved pain and he'd consider you weak if you didn't dare to embrace it as well. Retirement was nearing for him and he had been to the State Championship three times during his tenure, but failed to win each time. However, the Cedar Creek community thought this year could be a promising championship season because of the ten likely college recruits on the varsity football roster.

"Coach, I'm sorry but in all seriousness, you don't need to criticize us because you forgot to take your Viagra for your blow-up doll last night," Aaron shouted and smiled back at his teammates to chime in.

"Ha ha! Aaron, ohhhhh, Aaron... you're going to get it now." Travis, his close friend and the star quarterback, teased. His other close friend Reggie, who was the star running back, let out a chuckle and clapped his hands in excitement knowing that trouble was about to start. He gave Travis a nudge with his shoulder and impersonated the *Three Amigos Salute*.

"Get over here! All three of you, right now! You want to have a little fun, eh? Well... then we will. I and you three little punks are going to play what I call 'the slap game.'" Edwards yelled.

"But, I didn't…" Reggie stammered.

"Shut your fucking mouth! I've been dealing with your bullshit since you guys somehow managed to get past middle school. I don't care if you score touchdowns for my team. You are not going to disobey me like that," Edwards bickered as all three took off their helmets and crept over to their coach like snails on death row.

"What's he going to do make us run three miles?" Reggie whispered to his two buddies.

"I heard that. And after we finish this game here, you three can reward yourself with a three-mile victory lap with the pathetic track runners up there. I can assure you that *The Waterboy* Bobby Boucher won't be serving you H20 on a silver platter on the track either," Coach Edwards quipped.

After they all let out a groan, Aaron gave Reggie a violent shove. The rest of the team huddled around in a circle to watch their coach embarrass their teammates.

The summer heat engulfed the football practice field. Mercury muttered "fuck it, I'll raise two digits for the *hell* of it" and all thermometers in town raised from ninety-two to ninety-four. Across the street, the other side joyous side of reality existed. Heaven. Children were chirping away at a park playing in a splash pad, running around with super soakers and being spoon feed delicious refreshing watermelon and juice boxes. There was also an exhilarating comfort in knowing the park visit was only going to be fifteen minutes because it was way too damn hot to be there longer without any water. On school campus, high-school students were laughing and sneaking behind a construction area to get in the shade to smoke cigarettes. Teachers were discussing weekend plans and planning BBQs with their families. The blistering heat only fumigated Edwards and he knew it was time to declare himself the chief devil of this damn hell with his fifty subordinates.

"So, here's the deal. I'm going to slap each of you and then I will give you the opportunity to slap me back. My old coach back in high school did it to me too and it sure made me become more disciplined and win on the field." Edwards bragged.

The three shrugged and glanced at each other confused about what to expect next. Reggie stepped forward; Coach Edwards rubbed his hands together to create ferocious friction and slapped him right upside the head with no hesitation.

Reggie stumbled and stood in silence like a squandered scarecrow in sadistic shock. A huge red mark began to pulsate on the left side of his cheek while slow steady tears dripped down his face but quickly evaporated from the simmering sun. The rest of the team let out a gasp and whispered amongst each other. Reggie sighed and reluctancy walked back up to his coach who gave him the nod to return the favor. Reggie wound up and swung, but Coach Edwards flew his arm up and caught the attempt like a boa constrictor unleashing terror on a poor innocent mouse.

"You fucking pussy! You're too damn slow. And no, you don't get a second chance. Go! Take that three-mile run!" Coach Edwards screamed.

Reggie slowly picked up his helmet, held it towards his side and started jogging without saying a word to anyone. Aaron, Travis and the rest of the team watched in disbelief as Reggie trotted off into the distance. He combed back his long shaggy blonde hair and wiped tears from his face.

It was now Travis' turn to step up to the plate. He walked up cockily, raising his head toward his coach. Coach Edwards invited him to go first. Travis swung and Edwards immediately ducked the contact and returned a mean counter smack to his face Coach Edwards blew out through his nostrils like a rhino and simply pointed to the track.

Final up to bat was Aaron. His eyes glared pure evil and he was determined to show his coach he wasn't messing around. He huffed and puffed and stood with his chest out like Popeye, but hold the spinach, there was no time for spinach as an appetizer. It was time for a bloodbath

"You can get rid of that little pathetic 'bulldog' face you're trying to make. It doesn't impress me one bit. Now get closer so I can smack you to the other side of the Mississippi," Coach Edwards said.

Coach Edwards cocked back his right hand and connected with a strike to Aaron, that was more violent than the other two. As much as he liked Aaron on the field for how productive he was, he hated the fact that Aaron would often have the entire team turn against him simply for entertainment. After Aaron took the hit, he didn't even flinch. The teammates didn't say a word and stood in silence watching him crack his knuckles and brandish his fist as if it were a knife prepared to stab the head chief of this menacing hell on earth they called football practice.

Aaron stepped forward without any hesitation and dropped his hand sucker punching him with a closed fist right in the mouth. The ex-Navy Seal had been snipped himself. Aaron was pissed Edwards was always so hard on the football team. He felt Edwards had gone too far with his games and had to put him in his place. He looked down at his startled coach, shook his head in disgust and ran off to his other two buddies. Travis and Reggie were at the top of the hill with their jaws dropped.

Coach Edwards got to his feet and spit out a loogie of blood. "That son of a bitch sucker-punched me," he muttered to himself, holding his face in agony. He wiped the back of his hand across his lips and vividly stared at the red oozing liquid. He was in a trance for ten seconds. The head chief of hell was temporarily buried into his own grave. He looked over at his mesmerized team still huddled in a circle around him and screamed, "What the fuck are you all looking at? Hit the showers!"

Aaron bolted as fast as a cheetah hunting down a prey to meet up with Travis and Reggie. After catching them, he put his hands on his knee pads gasping for air. The three of them let out a chuckle and turned towards the practice field watching Coach Edwards bitch about the incident to the dumbfounded assistant coaches.

"All I have to say is 'Wow! That was incredible!' How the fuck did you manage to do that?" Travis' eyes were almost popping out of his skull in excitement.

"Man, you better not be suspended for the Homecoming game—that would blow a big one. But, props for that shit. There is absolutely no way that will ever happen on our campus again. I wish I would have been up close like everyone else though," Reggie chuckled in delight.

"Yeah, yeah, yeah will see. He deserved that punch for insulting all of us like that. I mean, he just went way overboard this time," Aaron said.

Fweeeeeeh! The loud noise of a whistle came from a distance. All three glanced at each other and then peered down to the field where their coach was pointing his finger. He was completely mute, only pointing instructing them to move immediately. Coach Edwards smothered in sweat, leaned against the entrance of the high school. With his shades hovering over his bald head eagerly waiting for them to continue their jog, they groaned and finished their competitive run in separate paces, passing by track athletes take a cool-down break to quench their thirst with Cool Blue Gatorade. After Reggie crossed the three-mile mark, he let out a menacing roar and vomited on the track. Small pellets of puke glistened in his long shaggy hair under the burning heat while they headed back to the locker room.

***

Exhausted and sweaty after the three-mile run after practice, the three boys walked into the locker room together. They raced to the water fountain, and each took twenty-second turns gulping down water to quench their thirst. The three boys didn't dare to mention what they had just discussed on the running tracks; Coach Edwards' office door was cracked open. He was sipping on a Gatorade ravenous for the echoing of eavesdropping opportunities. At the top of the door was a yellow note with capital letters in green marker stating "ATWOOD, IN MY OFFICE AFTER YOUR GOLDEN SHOWER. COACH EDWARDS."

The locker room was enshrined with championship banners, trophies, plaques, current team posters and inspirational quotes. One always stood out to the team, the one hanging above the entrance to the shower area—"Perfection is not attainable, but if we chase perfection we can catch excellence," Vince Lombardi. Cedar Creek High School had previously been known juggernaut football high-school programs in the state of Wisconsin, but over the last couple of years, Coach Edwards hadn't been able to pull the team over the hump to a State Championship.

Cedar Creek was a bustling small town twenty-five miles east of Madison, WI hopping with ma and pa shops, tasty tavern burgers, home-baked pastries that no business in the city could compete with and reliable mechanics and repairmen. The town refused to allow a restaurant or retail chains because there was fear it would hinder the rich vibrant history. The entire community was considered hard-working and watched out for each other, considering everyone's family. Violence was non-existent and all were given a second chance if he or she made a trivial mistake.

Groves of cedar trees blossomed all the neighborhoods, "The World's Largest Cinnamon Roll," a sixty-foot sculpture of a tasty gooey bun welcomed locals back home and tourists and small parks were nestled across the town. In fact, many people registered their own property as parks so that there was always an opportunity to get together for games of corn hole, bocce ball, BBQs and firework shows regardless of the season. An autumn aerial view of the town's canopy would embrace a frolicking fall foliage; it was an un-be-leaf-able scene with vibrant seasonal paint strokes that ignited the entire community's dopamine levels.

The Cedar Creek flowed through the town from north to south and it was a ritual to pick berries that grew on the trees on the walking paths on the river. Some people were reluctant to visit the creek because of the folklore describing the entire river bed as an old ancient Indian burial ground. During the fall, several families would attend kid-friendly mini-Haunted houses with petting zoos, corn mazes, jack-o-lantern contests and pumpkin patches. Only the thrill-seekers were daring to show up in the evenings to attend bonfires dressed as goblins, witches, vampires, scarecrows and ghosts. Dubbed as 'Cedar Creep.' The adult agenda consisted of sharing chili, apple cider mixed with soda and sitting quietly to listen for the afterlife. Supposedly, more ghost sightings happening during the fall, so it eventually became a tradition for the town to frequently visit during that time period.

But, when it came to Friday nights during the fall, there were only maybe the spirits down by the creek. Many of the businesses closed early to tailgate for the Cedar Creek Silver Eagles football team. It was always pandemonium with everyone high-fiving and screaming their heads off in joyous glory. As a player, it was a privilege to be able to play for that town, because they always had your back and were going to raise the roof with noise no matter what the score was. On Friday mornings, the town started a synchronized wave from the north side to the south side. Everyone would sit on their patios with their coffees, omelets, toast, hash browns and raise their arms in delight as the wave came their way. Some argued that Cedar Creek football was three times more diehard than any Texas high-school football program.

Travis and Reggie pointed towards the note on Edwards' door. Aaron replied with a silent nod and let out a sigh while opening up the door to his locker for a towel and Ocean Breeze Suave shampoo. Inside every locker door, every player had a tapped rabbit's foot for good luck and pictures of Green Bay Packers memorabilia. Anyone that rooted against the Packers would frequently be the victim of wet towel whipping on Mondays if their favorite team somehow miraculously beat the "Green and Gold." Aaron graciously brushed the rabbit's foot seven times for good measure and slouched his back against his locker room door to let out a heavy moan in frustration.

"Shit. Man, give me a call after you're done with Coach. Maybe the three of us can catch a game of pool at The Lucid Owl later?" whispered Travis.

"Yeah, I'll let you know." Aaron and miserably walked over to the shower. The hot water splashed across his face as he rested his arms against the wall. He stared at his knuckles and winced. Blood from his idiotic yet triumphant punch to his coach leaked into the drain. He rubbed his eyes with his fists—flashes of vibrant colors in the shapes of Rubik's cubes appeared. He continued to rub his eyes and pictured himself running towards the end zone after breaking a tackle. Continuing to run, the crowd cheered as he neared the goal line. Right after, Coach Edwards' face appeared and blew fire like a hideous dragon rolling his head back roaring with demonic laughter He quickly opened his eyes and turned off the shower. An eerie silence surrounded the locker room; he knew it was time to face the music.

Aaron grabbed his towel off the rack, wiped himself down, and looked in the mirror while shaking his head. He stood there looking at his hazel eyes, neatly trimmed goatee, freckles and the swelling on his cheek from the confrontation earlier. Out of all the players, he was in the best shape—he started to lift weights when he was only thirteen. His full name was Aaron Avery Atwood and not surprisingly his nickname was "Triple A." He also had the adrenaline of the Energizer Bunny and expertise in mechanics. No one in his family needed a AAA membership with him around—he could change tires, brake pads and do oil changes with ease. It must have been the unlimited supply of AAA Duracell in his bloodstream.

The hard work ethic didn't come easily though. It took a lot of discipline from his family. That was why he admired his brother, Tyler. They would always go to the gym together to lift weights, run up and down the one hundred staircases outside the local library and every morning muster down a shake that had spinach, Greek yogurt, wild frozen blueberries specifically from Maine, carrots, bananas, turmeric, black pepper, cinnamon, almond milk and vanilla bean protein powder. Tyler was an All State wide receiver heavily recruited, but his opportunity was cut short after tearing his ACL. Aaron would often promise Tyler—who was now a lawyer—that he'd win a championship to make up for the dreadful day he got injured in the first quarter of a State Championship game five years earlier.

Aaron scrubbed down his head, dropped the towel and put his fists together. He envisioned himself as Rocky Balboa boxing Coach. He let out a smirk, slammed his hands on the sink and walked over to his locker. He put on his University of Wisconsin sweatpants and a hooded sweatshirt. The goal was to enroll with the Badgers after graduating high school to possibly play football or basketball. He felt he, Travis and Reggie had a shot at being part of their athletic programs. No matter what happened with scholarship opportunities, they all agreed to room together; Reggie had relatives who lived around the Madison area and rented out houses to college students.

"Aaron? I'm waiting. I don't have all night. I have to be back here early tomorrow morning for a staff meeting!" Coach Edwards said loudly from the office. "Naked? Ha ha. It was *A Streetcar Named Desire*, you fool!" He continued to yell while looking at the television.

"Coming, coming, coming. Be there in a second!" Aaron yelled back. He threw his dirty uniform and towel in his duffel bag, and hurried to Coach's office. It was all or nothing. In the back of Aaron's mind was the very least a two-game suspension. If that was indeed his punishment, he'd be ineligible to play in the anticipated Homecoming game against their biggest rival, the Edgewater Crusaders.

"Close the door, please." Coach Edwards spun around his chair from watching *Wheel of Fortune*.

"Wow, what a beautiful trip you won there to Buenos Aires for your family. I hope your golden retriever puppy, Mickey can still be invited for the trip if he leaves the socks and the need for surgery alone," Pete Sajak, the show's host, joked to the contestant. Coach Edwards flipped the television off without looking at the remote in his hand.

"I'm really sorry, Coach. My emotions got the best of me. I was just upset that you were insulting my friends like that," Aaron said.

"Just sit down, Atwood." Edwards snapped back sitting cross-legged with one finger placed on the side of his face. Aaron nodded grabbing at his goatee and took a seat on the chair straight across from his angry bitter coach. The office sported an Ireland flag, pictures of leprechauns, exquisite portraits of the Cliffs of Moher and The Rock of Cashel and a family tree displaying Edwards' African Irish heritage.

"You know what? You got a lot of balls, kid. And, truthfully, I respect the hell out of you for what you did."

"You do? But I…"

"Just shut up for a second, Aaron. I'm trying to speak here. See, that's what I hate… what you guys are doing. I can't stand when people interrupt others; it fucking pisses me off. Trust me, I understand you guys enjoy pranks more than anyone. I'm fine with that. Do that in the classroom or off school grounds. But my football field, our football field I should say…. is no playground. Capeesh?" Edwards picked up a Rubik's cube from his knick-knack collection on the desk.

"I understand, Coach. It's just difficult going through an eight-hour day having fun at school with my friends. I mean, not all fun. I'm learning and passing my classes. Otherwise, I wouldn't have the opportunity to be here. But, after school is out, the fun is over and it seems like we're clocking in to work here. But we don't get a pay stub," Aaron said.

"Stop right there with that bullshit. That's what you have yet to learn. R-E-S-P-O-N-S-I-B-I-L-I-T-Y," Edwards spelled out. "If you want to make it big anywhere, you must control your urges, mature in this world and earn some credibility. Yes, I understand you're so young and just want to have fun, but sooner or later you're going to learn it's time to shape up. On the other hand, you have a gift. You are great at persuading people and at doing great things. Unfortunately, most of the time you are convincing them to do things they shouldn't. I need you to be more vocal in a positive way and persuade your teammates to help us find that pesky little Leprechaun. Gold. It's right on that damn football field. I know you guys are craving a championship as much as I am. All we have to do is find the other side of the fucking rainbow." Coach Edwards twirled the Rubik's cube on the table next to a bowl of root beer hard candies; a treat he depended on to distract himself from his cigarette cravings when he was under heavy stress.

Aaron raised his hand to speak and Edwards barked back, "Good. Now I got your attention. However, this is damn football. Not school. You don't need to raise your hand to speak your mind."

"I'm feeling you, Coach. My parents give me this talk all the time about school. It is about time I really consider looking toward my future. I'll help take lead and get the boys back into gear. Winning a championship would help us both tremendously. I really want to play for Wisconsin and I think we can do it with our team's chemistry this year."

"Ha ha. Good! Great! Grand! Just keep your pranks to a minimum and stay out of trouble. Don't let me return the favor of a black eye," Edwards laughed. "I didn't know you had it in you. Now, I just want you to repeat that aggression every day on the football field and yell at your teammates on the field. You can get in their heads more than anyone out there. Now go home, eat your dinner, do your homework and catch some Zzzs."

"I have to be honest, Coach. I've never seen this side of you. I was totally expecting you to suspend me for my actions out there earlier."

"Do to others what you would like to be done to you. It's called the 'Golden Rule.' Follow that and you will be on the right track." Edwards popped a root beer hard candy in his mouth and twirled it around with his tongue

"Thanks, Coach. I appreciate the advice. Have a good one." Aaron shook his coach's hand, grabbed a hard candy for himself and smirked as his Coach opened the door.

"Aaron! Wait," Edwards yelled. Aaron turned around to face Coach opening up his mini refrigerator to grab a Gatorade and pretended to punt it in the air letting out a chuckle for his actions earlier. He pump-faked and then tossed it over and gave him a salute. Aaron saluted back and walked out in the parking lot to his maroon 94' Oldsmobile Cutlass Supreme. He opened up his car's door, started the engine and muttered "What a crock of shit!"

CHAPTER 2

"Ta ta ta psh psh da da ta ta psh psh reeva reeva roo roo."
Aaron beatboxed pretending to scratch records, then reached to
his backseat for a nice cold Coors Lite. The Cutlass had the
passenger rear-view mirror dangling like a door stopper, a
spider web crack in the windshield from a large piece of ice
had been thrown on it and the backseat smothering in stink
from McDonald's McGriddle wrappers and socks that hadn't
been washed in weeks. Pewwww! Plugging his nose in disgust,
he knew a vacuum and car wash was mandatory and would
have preferred being sprayed by a skunk over the custom-made
Little Trees car freshener he invented. He cracked open his
beer, took a huge chug and nodded his head with gratitude
about the refreshing taste he was enduring. He pulled up to a
stoplight a few blocks from the school, set the beer in the
console and tapped his hands against the wheel. As he awaited
the DJ to announce the next song, he kept looking in the rear-
view mirror for cops.

"Ladies and gents! DJ Stunt here. Y'all know what's
dropping down low, don't you? It's 7 o'clock on Thirsty
Thursday. Y'all know what that means, folks. We got the top
seven songs coming your way. Y'all know if you are the

seventh caller, you got yo'self the winning prize. I'll be revealing the giveaway in just a bit. But ahhhh… yeah, here we go with the seventh song. It's time to get your drink on and start enjoying this weeeee weeeee weeee-kennnnnddddd!"

Aaron raised his beer to give the DJ Stunt's comments a toast and took another sip from his beer. Looking into the broken passenger rear-view mirror, he noticed his science teacher who was currently failing him. The teacher looked at him with a repulsive face, and signaled her finger to pull over so she could give him a lecture. She was a young, petite big-breasted woman with blonde frizzy hair who—she had just recently finished from grad school. Students would secretly sing the song, "Oh me, oh my. She's a slice of grandma's cinnamon home-baked apple pie, the grand finale on Fourth July, the metamorphosis of a spotted autumn butterfly. Oh Andrei, let me sing you a lullaby and pour you some whisky rye," if they saw her in the hallway.

"Holy fuck! Mrs. Gleason? No fucking way!" Aaron screamed. He quickly rolled up the window and turned his head the other way. The light turned green; he switched gears, put the pedal to the metal and sped off splashing beer on his face. As he licked his chin, he sported a menacing grin and pulled ferociously at his thick brown goatee like a cat clawing scratching at the kitchen door salivating for some scrumptious salmon.

"Ha ha ha! There is no way this shit is happening. Now I'm definitely not passing science class! Ha ha ha!" Aaron looked over his shoulder and noticed that Mrs. Gleason was following him. She had her window rolled down and was yelling out for Aaron to stop. Aaron rolled down his window and yelled back to her.

"Hey, Mrs. Gleason! Nice to see you! I have to hurry back to my family for dinner. C-ya tomorrow!" Aaron gleamed with sarcasm. The *chemistry* wasn't working between them; Mrs. Gleason lost her patience and blasted the horn.

"Jesus! What does this bitch want? All I had was one fucking man soda. One beer!" Aaron was startled back and began to get paranoid. He let out a sigh, put both hands on the wheel and knew it was time to escape. Ms. Gleason was now tailgating Aaron down the local country road. Aaron looked over his shoulder, turned his blinker on to go left and then quickly bolted right into a cornfield. Mrs. Gleason—who had turned left—quickly stopped on the brakes and got out of the car shielding her eyes from the hot beaming sun looking into the cornfield.

Swoosh! Swoosh! Swoosh! Cornstalks flew up in the air as he drove into the field laughing like a hyena. To get rid of the evidence, he smashed the beer car and threw it out the window. The hole of the beer landed on top of a corn stalk that was still upright right next to a bridge crossing Cedar Creek. Panicking, Aaron realized he didn't follow the superstition of holding your breath while passing a cemetery, which to many the entire creek was considered. The consequence was being possessed by evil spirits.

Wiping sweat from his forehead at a fork in the road, he heard his police radar go off and quickly slowed down, turned on his directional, pulled down a culdesack and parked the car. As an act of subterfuge, he nonchalantly grabbed his backpack, got out of the car and walked down the street as if he didn't own the vehicle. On one knee, Aaron pretended to tie his shoe before a police officer slowly passed by; he was drinking a cup of Dunkin Donuts coffee and nodded friendly. Close call! The officer turned out of sight and Aaron ran back to his car in fear that Mrs. Gleason was going to unleash chemical elements from the Periodic Table on him. A cocktail of Polonium, Mercury and Arsenic would certainly grant an "F" as a science experiment. "F" as in flatlined.

"Fuck! Fuck! Fuck!" Aaron let out a shriek; his car keys were in the ignition. The engine was still running, but he was locked out of the car. He kicked at the driver's door and lowered his shoulder into it, but nothing.

"Ha! What a fucking great way to start the upcoming weekend," Aaron muttered to himself while putting the other strap of the back on. "At least I didn't have that much gas left. Well, I hope anyway." Aaron darted through backyards to get to his house—a mile run didn't seem too bad. Playing a game of espionage, he looked each way as he crossed streets to make sure Mrs. Gleason wasn't still searching for him.

Meanwhile, while Mrs. Gleason tried to keep pace with Aaron, she fumbled through her students' directory of emergency contact information. She found Aaron's house address and scrolled her index finger past it.

"That little bastard. He's going to finally get it now," Mrs. Gleason said as she let out a sigh and entered Aaron's address into her GPS system. Mrs. Gleason slowly and steadily typed 2820 Dunwoody Avenue. She followed each direction and ended up at his house, but noticed there was no Cutlass Supreme in the driveway as she pulled up. She sat there for a second deciding if she would wait a bit and looked at her beautiful hazel eyes and dimple in the mirror.

"Clever one. Hiding at his friend's house." Mrs. Gleason shook her head in disgust. Panting heavily, Aaron turned the corner to his street and noticed Mrs. Gleason's Honda Civic in his driveway. He abruptly dove into the nearest bushes and his head hit on a lawn gnome.

"Fuck!" Aaron yelled in pain and quickly covered his mouth. Laying in the grass, he watched Mrs. Gleason light up a cigarette, back out of the driveway and take off. Did she already pay a visit to his parents? Aaron brushed his pants off and ran across the street to his house.

"Get the hell off my front lawn!" Mr. Donaldson, his neighbor who was overprotective of the quality of his lawn, said. He was a retired old stubborn man who would spend four hours a day on his yard. Opening up *Golf's Digest* one would point their finger at a golf course and wonder whether or not it was Mr. Donaldson's yard. The backyard was a wonderland filled with a garden, fire pit patio, twenty-foot-high gazebo, several exotic trees, pond with several breeds of fish and a three-hole golf course. He also owned an English Mastiff named Toro who howled at anyone that came near five feet of his property. It had become a tradition for teenagers to frequently liter his yard with baseballs that had riddles written on them. But, these ones were dirtier than the ones found on

Laffy Taffy candy wrappers. The tradition supposedly started because Toro resembled Hercules, who was the same dog in *The Sandlot.* Perhaps, the teenagers only started the trend because Mr. Donaldson was a huge asshole overly anal about his property.

Question: I go in hard but come out soft, and I never mind if you want to blow me. What am I? Answer: Chewing gum.

"Sorry, Mr. Donaldson! I fell!" Aaron yelled back to his neighbor.

"No, you didn't, you damn liar! If I catch you in my yard again, I'm calling the cops on you. You hear me?" Mr. Donaldson shrieked back as Aaron closed the door to his home and wiped the sweat off his face from the mile trek.

"You stink, Aaron. Why didn't you shower after practice?" Aaron's mother Donna asked. She plugged her nose as the family dog—one-year-old golden retriever Teddy—jumped on Aaron to greet him.

"All the guys used up the hot water. Plus, I just love bringing the aroma of football practice back to the house. You know that, Mom," Aaron sarcastically replied and pet Teddy who was wagging his tail whimpering in excitement glad to see him home.

"And uh, where's your car?" Austin, Aaron's dad, questioned looking out the window. He frowned glaring his eyebrows, turning to his son and folding his arms waiting for an answer. "Well?"

"Uh, Reggie had to borrow it. He ran out of gas, so he dropped me off here and now he's going to get gas and fill his car up. His dad is going to follow him with my car and drop it off later."

"I doubt Jimmy [Reggie's dad] is going to appreciate that favor," Austin replied back sharply.

"I hope that's all he's doing with your car. Remember, I just filled that gas tank up yesterday for you," Donna said.

"Yeahhhh, that's all he's doing with it, Mom. I have to shower quickly though," Aaron said as he walked towards the basement door.

"Okay. Hurry up with your shower. We're having your favorite—barbecue pork sandwiches. And don't stink up that basement. I just cleaned it an hour ago, Aaron!" Donna yelled and laughed.

"I'm not hungry now. I'll warm leftovers up later tonight." Aaron ran down the stairs to his newly refurbished basement.

His parents had saved up some money to remodel it and create another bedroom for Aaron—he did not have to share a room with his younger brother Jason anymore. His parents were both bright-minded teachers working in a separate school district from their children. They were heavily involved in the Booster Club for Aaron's high school.

"You really did work down here, Ma. But cool with the apple cinnamon scent eh? We're not in fall just yet." Aaron yelled back up.

"Funny, Aaron, funny," his mother muttered at the top of the stairs.

Aaron opened up his pocket to retrieve his cell phone. He went into his room, locked the door and started to dial Reggie. Aaron desperately needed some help; his car was running and the gas tank was full. He didn't want to have to ask his parents to get out of this predicament. Ring... ring... ring... ring...

"Come on you fucker, pick up!" Aaron said to himself.

"What's up, douche bag?" Reggie responded with laughter in his tone.

"Yo Reggie. I need your help. I locked my car on Starin Road and the gas is running. Can you pick me up?"

"Why the hell do you have your car there for, dumbass? Ha-ha!" Reggie snickered.

"Mrs. Gleason caught me with a cold one on the way back from practice and has been stalking me."

"Well, fuck man. That ain't good. Are you going to get shit for that you think?" Reggie asked.

"Fuck it. I don't know dude. Can you just do me this favor?" Aaron begged.

"Nah, sorry bro. Yeah, I know it sounds bad but I'm running errands with my mom."

"Wow. You're pathetic. Momma's boy. Whatever. I'll call you later," Aaron hung up the phone and slammed his hands on the kitchen sink. An apple cinnamon scented Glade plugin fell out of the outlet and rolled his eyes displeased with the sequence of bad luck.

He sniffed his armpits and plugged his nose. Glade wouldn't dare to make a scent off his pungent body odor or the inside of the Cutlass. Hell, even The Jelly Belly Candy Company would wave the white towel before committing to making a funky, prank flavor based on his stench. He rubbed himself down with deodorant, quickly changed into running clothes and headed upstairs.

"Teddyyyyyyy!" Aaron screamed as he reached the top of the stairs. His pup, Teddy, frantically barked and came running from the kitchen where he was begging for some of the dinner being prepped. Teddy—with the leash in his mouth— jumped up to Aaron and tail whipped the side of the wall like an uncontrollable bulldozer.

"Good boy," Aaron said praising Teddy and petting his head. "Mom! I'm going for a run with Teddy. I'll be back in a bit," Aaron yelled out to the kitchen.

Aaron put the collar on Teddy and walked into the laundry room where the family house and car keys hung. Peaking over his shoulder, he watched to see if anyone was coming into the room. He snatched the spare key to his car, sneakily put it in his pocket, walked outside and let out a sigh of relief. Aaron attached his phone to his arm, put his headphones on, and began the trek to his car with Teddy.

As his neighbors worked on their Wisconsin suburban lawns, Aaron waved back and kept running. Closing his eyes, he visualized he was on the football field in the state championship game and had caught the game-winning touchdown opportunity. The defense was getting closer, and he throttled up a jetpack to avoid a last-second tackle. Within thirty seconds, he had reached the endzone; his Cutlass Supreme.

"Come on, Teddy! Let's go!" Aaron screamed at his dog fumbling to take off his headphones. Teddy began to whimper and back paddled from the car—he didn't want the fun and games to end just yet.

"I'm sorry, pup. I'll make the next run a lot longer. Now, get in the car, boy," Aaron coaxed whistling at him. Ring….ring….ring… ring… Aaron reached in the pocket of his sweatpants. Looking at his phone, his friend Travis was calling him.

"Yo dude, I'm kind of busy. I'll call you back in a bit," Aaron shouted as he fiercely held onto Teddy who was trying to continue to scamper away while whimpering.

"Yeah. Well… you could have asked me to give you a lift to your car. Ha-Ha. Reggie told me about Gleason. That bitch. That's a bummer man." Travis laughed back.

"Yeah, it fucking blows, but I thought you were with Angela. Listen, I have to go. I'll call you later on tonight."

"Sounds good. Thirsty Thursday tonight. Alright alright alright," Travis mimicked Matthew McConaughey's signature phrase.

"Ha. Peace McConaughey." Aaron reached to put his phone back in his pocket; Teddy got lose and took off like a lightning bolt down barking with delight.

"That's it! I'm calling the vet to get your balls cut once I finally catch you," he screamed running back towards his car. "One thing after another. This is getting fucking ridiculous," Aaron muttered to himself hopping into his car. As he swerved around the corner, Reggie and his mom were driving around the bend in their Honda CR-V.

"Slow down, Aaron! You're driving like an idiot! You're going to kill someone driving like that," Reggie's mom shouted out the window as they both approached each other in the street.

"I'm trying to catch Teddy. He ran away." Aaron slammed on his brakes.

"Okay, we will help you. But slow down! Head down Lake Street and I'll meet you on Main Street at the corner." Reggie's mother said.

"Andale. Ariba!" Reggie screamed imitating cartoon character *Speedy Gonzalez* hitting the passenger side of the car as if he was a jockey trying to make his horse go faster.

Reggie's mom, Rita, pulled into a driveway and turned around to go back in the direction she and Reggie came from. Aaron leaned his head out the window as he desperately searched for Teddy.

Ruff! Ruff! Ruff! Aaron turned the corner to see Teddy hosting a mischievous solo parade bolting down the street with his tongue flailing. As he turned the corner, Reggie and his mom were turning as well to meet at their destined rendezvous. Beeeeeeppppp! Reggie's mom's tires screeched as she tried to put her car to a halt. She almost hit Teddy. Ruff! Ruff! Ruff! Teddy ran up to their car and leaped up on their window to greet them; he then began scratching at their windows to try to get inside their car. Reggie's mom lowered the window— Teddy jumped in their car and began licking Reggie's face.

"Ha ha! Teddy! You naughty pup! Hey, Aaron! Come here! We got him. We got him," Reggie screamed as Teddy continued to lick his face with excitement. Aaron pulled up and parked right next to Reggie to make Teddy's transfer easier.

"Rita, thank you so much for your help. I really appreciate it," Aaron said as he rested his hands on top of the roof of her car—he stood by her side of the window.

"You're welcome, Aaron. Just try to maintain that pup. He's one of those rare feisty goldens. So, what are your guys' big plans tonight?" Rita asked looking back and forth at both of the boys.

"No idea yet. Maybe will watch the Brewers game at my place," Aaron said—he knew at the back of his mind that idea wasn't their intention.

"Yeah I'll bring the chips and guacamole," Reggie added.

"You better finish your paper before you do anything. You guys have to realize this is the big year. Staying out late on weekdays is no cure for "senioritis." If you want to get accepted to Wisconsin, you have to focus a bit more on your studies."

"We'll see, Mom, will see. I just like seeing my B.A.C. slightly higher than my G.P.A. on a consistent basis." Reggie laughed.

"You guys are goofballs. Just hope you two don't get caught doing your underage drinking. Anyway, I'd like to stay and chat a bit more here in the middle of the road, but I just don't see that happening. I got laundry to take care of. Have to get the brown streaks out of Reggie's underwear. Good luck with Teddy, Aaron. Tell your mother I say hi." Rita smirked and gave Aaron a wave. Reggie and Aaron both laughed.

"Call me once you're ready to get something going tonight," Reggie said as they drove off.

Aaron pulled into his driveway, turned off the car and pressed his head against the wheel letting everything that had happened in the past few hours sink in. A torturous day in the inferno of Hell. From sucker punching his coach, Mrs. Gleason catching him drink a beer, crossing over an Indian burial ground without holding his breath, and almost losing his dog, it was almost as if he signed a death warrant before he went to bed last night. Aaron let out a sigh, brought Teddy into the house and walked past his parents watching *The Weather Channel*.

"It might storm for your game tomorrow night, Son," Aaron's father said pointing at the television and shoving popcorn down his mouth. "Make sure you wash your football pants tonight too. They have huge grass stains on them."

"Yeah I will," Aaron said softly and headed down the basement.

"What's with you? You seem so bummed out. Did Teddy wear you out on that run?" his mother asked concerned.

"Ha. Yeah. I'm a little exhausted but I think I'm going to go to Travis's to watch the baseball game tonight," Aaron replied.

"Don't stay out too late. You have to get some rest. Don't be stupid and be waking up with a hangover tomorrow morning. This is an important game," Aaron's dad yelled with a mouthful of popcorn in his mouth. Austin had a very strict personality and was adamant that his three sons were always on the right path to a successful life. He had a military background, was very muscular, and standing he was 6' 6" tall. He had a pointed chin, shaved head and tattoos all over his body.

Aaron got to his basement, shook his head, threw his dirty socks in the corner and flicked his dad off from the bottom of the stairs without him seeing the dirty gesture. He would often do so when he was upset about his dad's constant yelling at him. It could be for a chore he had not done, underage drinking and not making responsible choices when it came to his potential future scholarship opportunities. For Aaron, It was time to let off some much-needed stress and grab a few beers with the guys before their game tomorrow night. After showering and putting on his fresh pair of socks, he reached the very back left corner of his sock drawer and pulled out his fake I.D.

"You better do some magic tonight, Douglas," Aaron told himself holding the fake I.D. [of Douglas] up to his face. Aaron had gotten all of their fakes from Travis's older brother. They each paid $50.00 to get one made and had to sign a contract confirming that they would never rat him out if they ever got caught by parents, teachers or the police.

Aaron dialed up Travis on the line who immediately snickered. "You finally ready? Jeez man, what'd you have to deal with, your period?"

"Good one, dumb ass. No, I had a lot of bullshit to deal with this evening. You going to pick me up?" Aaron asked as he combed and spiked up his short brown hair flexing his muscles in the mirror.

"Yup, just finishing my SHube. I'll be there in fifteen minutes." He flexed as he put aftershave over his face and started to make poses. "God, I'm fucking sexy," he exclaimed as he continued to admire himself in the mirror— the exact thing Aaron was doing. SHube was their codeword for men getting ready: Shit, Shower, Shave. The SH for the first two letters and the SHube short for cube to signify the 3D aspect of it being an alliteration of three words.

Travis was the most well-dressed of the three; he was known as the ladies man because he was the star quarterback for the football team. Despite always flirting with the girls and occasionally upsetting his long-time girlfriend, Angela, he would never cheat on her. Angela, a junior was pretty tight with the three guys—they had known each other since grade school. Travis was always neatly shaven. He had spiked blonde hair, dark blue eyes and a noticeable scar on the right side of his face from a car accident when he was younger. His father would always tell him, "Kissing models are always clean-shaven," which prompted him to shave twice every day.

"Ha-ha. Shut the hell up. Don't bring Angela either. It's a boy's night out. No girlfriends. Call Reggie too and pick him up after me," Aaron said.

"Girlfriends? I don't think it's plural in our scenario." Travis laughed as he buttoned up his polo t-shirt, scratched his head and let out a yawn.

"Tired, you pussy? Ha-ha. Whatever. I'll see you in a jiffy," Aaron said and he put on a pair of his Aeropostale jeans and threw three sticks of Wrigley Juicy Fruit gum in his mouth. The call disconnected and Travis dialed Reggie.

"Yo. Aaron just texted me. I'm busy helping my mom with the groceries. When are you going to be here?" Reggie asked as he flipped his brown shaggy blonde hair back. Reggie was bulkier than the others; his teammates called him "The Dead End" because he could break tackles by running people over. He occasionally also played tight end and was a great blocker and he never allowed a sack.

"Why the hell did he tell me to call you then? Alright. Whatever. I'll be there in twenty or so," Travis proclaimed and squirted some cologne on.

"Peace—" Reggie abruptly hung up.

Reggie ran up to his room and changed into his Milwaukee Brewers buttoned-up jersey. He was an avid fan of all the Wisconsin sports team and would constantly be wearing jerseys and other sports memorabilia at school. He squirted on some of his Nike cologne and ran downstairs to turn on *Sportscenter*.

"I was watching something in there, Reggie." Reggie's mother yelled from inside the kitchen.

Beep! Beep! Beep! "Fine, whatever. Travis is here anyway," Reggie replied switching the channel back to the *Home Shopping Network.* Beeeeeeep! Beeeeeeep! Beeeeeeeeeep! Travis honked the horn as loud and as many times as he could to simply annoy Reggie and his mother.

"What an idiot!" Reggie's mother scolded while chopping up vegetables for a salad.

"Yup, he sure is." Reggie reached around his mom to grab his wallet off the counter. He gave her a salute with a little smirk and ran out the door to Aaron and Travis blasting *Duck Down* by The Roots as they rocked the car back and forth like it was a boat. They called it the "earthquake" and it became the high-school trend in parking lots. From a bird eyes' view, one would witness brown paper bags, stereos elevating to an unimaginable decibel and cars rocking to a Richter Scale—a geologist would shit his pants if he calculated the metrics of the earthquake in Cedar Creek High School's parking lot. The predicted magnitude was always 10.0, the street address of the high school.

"You guys are ridiculous! My mom was having a riot in there." Reggie laughed and hopped in the backseat of the 1998 Buick Skylark.

"Ha-ha! What did that hottie say?" Travis chuckled and turned the music down a tad; he then looked back at Reggie tossing Travis's dirty trash collection of laundry, Gatorade bottles filled with chew spit, fast food bags and homework assignments to make more room.

"Fuck you, dude. Looks like someone got a D on Mrs. Gleason's geology exam?" Reggie gave Travis a light punch in the shoulder.

"You little bitch," Travis snapped back and rubbed his shoulder.

"Awwwww. You two having a little fight? Please, don't have your make-up make-out session in front of me, you douche bags." Aaron chimed in.

"Ha-Ha. Whatever. Anyway, when the hell are you going to clean your car up, Travis?" Reggie asked as he still was trying to organize Travis's textbooks, football clothing and other foreign object debris.

"Ha-ha. Yeah, I should probably take care of that. Angela has been bitching about it to me too. But, enough talking. We have plenty of time to shoot the shit at the bar. Let's get ready to rage and rock out, boys!" Travis hollered, turned the music up and hovered down a hopeful highway of harmony in his Honda.

CHAPTER 3

Shenanigans, pandemonium and debauchery held hands and jumped in unison into a blender to catapult the evening for the three young gents. It was going to be their first time using their fake I.D.s to get into the local bar. They had been in taverns before, but they either knew the bouncer or had to sneak in. They were expecting red carpet treatment and were certain they would remember this moment for the rest of their lives.

"There she is," Aaron pointed at The Lucid Owl, the bar's parking lot they were pulling into.

"Hell yea!" Reggie gave his approval to Aaron. Travis lowered the loud heavy metal music and parked the Buick in the farthest spot from the entrance of the bar—just in case they had to flee from being rejected with their fakes. Aaron and Reggie were about to open their car doors, but instead, Travis pushed the lock button.

"Wait," Travis preached. "We have to make a toast for this shit, man. I mean… we're going to remember this forever. You always remember your firsts in everything. Your first bitch, first car, first bloody brawl, first touchdown. This will be our first bar night out with our fakes." Travis said in excitement.

"Man, you couldn't have said it any better," Aaron replied back nodding his head in approval, all amped up ready for this experience.

"I was thinking the same thing, boys. That's why I brought three silos for us to shotgun before we go in there," Reggie said and pulled the three frosty cold PBR's from his pocket.

"You're a fucking genius, my man." Aaron gave Reggie a fist pump.

Reggie handed Travis and Aaron their beer and pulled out his butterfly knife from his pocket. He jammed a hole with the knife in all three beers—they all clinked their cans together, put the shotgunned cans to their mouths and slammed them in five seconds. Reggie grabbed the empty beer cans and buried them under Travis's garbage in his backseat.

"Ahhhhh. That went down way too damn good. That means it's going to be one hell of a night," Aaron said.

"Amen to that," Reggie nodded, rubbed his hands together and grinned in delight.

They all took out their fakes for one more fateful peak. Reggie held his high in the air and Aaron and Travis flashed a smile and touched their I.D.'s to promote good fortune and signify their passage inside. They reached the entrance and were greeted by a tall, overweight, bald-headed bouncer with a very large thick goatee that was down to his belly button.

The Lucid Owl was a local dive bar that was filled with exotic sculptures and antiques; some of the items included a large grandfather clock, grand piano, lava lamps, non-ancient Mayan hieroglyphic scriptures carved into the wall and a large dream catcher hanging above the bar. Five hammocks were available to any patron to take a snooze, meditate or a drunken slumber; the name of the bar did promote lucid dreaming after all. At the very front of the bar, there was a six-foot statue of an owl that sprung its head around at the top of every hour and hooted at last call—the owners were an older couple from Argentina who were former holistic doctors that always had an interest of creating a bar with a spa-like atmosphere. The preview of the Brewers baseball game was being played on one small TV from the 70's sporting bunny ears. There were posters of all the Cedar Creek current high school sports teams. The bouncer sat next to a picture of the Silver Eagles football team. Hopefully, he wouldn't notice the three from the picture. Maybe he never bothered to ever even look at it.

"I.D.s please," the bouncer grunted and scratched the nape of his neck. Each of them flashed their I.D.s. He slowly studied each of them by shifting his face from the ID and back to the face several times. All of them stayed confident and looked into the bouncer's eyes as he gave hesitant looks. "Okay, you guys are good. Come on in. I don't remember you guys being here before but we started a new special on Thursdays. It's $10 all you can drink domestic cans," the bouncer said as he pointed at the advertisement on the wall. He then cracked his knuckles and twirled his finger in his long bushy blonde goatee.

"Thanks," all three of them said and walked with the biggest grins on their faces. Finally, it was time to distress. No scolding parents, no nagging coaches, no chores, no homework. They gave each other an excited shove and pulled out their wallets scrambling for an Alex Hamilton to cover the special, and an Abraham Lincoln to cover a tip for the bartender.

"Damn, that bartender is a smoke show," Aaron said dropping his jaw and trying to avoid staring at her.

"What can I get for you guys?" the bartender said with a blush on her face. She was a petite woman with blonde hair and her phone in between her breasts. She had a nose piercing

—super sexy to the three boys. Wait, they weren't boys anymore. They were now men enjoying some nice cold ones on a thirsty Thursday evening.

"Hey there, sweetie. I think we all are going to do the special," Reggie said while giving her a little wink and laying money on the bar.

"Ha-ha. Alrighty, what are you guys drinking? For the special, it's the choice of PBR, Coors Lite, Miller Lite or Bud Lite." The bartender rested her hand on her chin and elbows on the bar.

"Definitely a PBR," Travis chimed in. "By the way, what's your name?"

"My name is Kimberly and I'll be here all night to close for you guys. I think we might be doing a karaoke contest tonight if you guys are interested in signing up?"

"Ha-ha. Will see. Will see. Liquor encouragement may make us do it." Aaron laughed and drummed his hands on the barstool.

"Ha-ha. It is quite a sight for Kegaroke nights," Kimberly said and reached down in the fridge to grab three frosty cold cans of PBR.

"Kegaroke?" Aaron asked as he grabbed the beer from Kimberly. "Thanks."

"Yup, Kegaroke. We do it every other Thursday night if we draw a big enough crowd. First place wins a free keg party on any Saturday night they want."

"That's awesome. Might have to try to win that." Reggie opened his beer and took a nice gulp.

"Ha. Yeah right, Reggie. You suck at singing. If anyone is going to win, it's going to be me." Travis bragged as he pointed his thumb to his chest.

"Ha-ha. You guys are funny. It sure looks like you're getting ready for the stage quick the way you're slamming those beers." Kimberly laughed as she reached out and grabbed Reggie's can to measure how much was left.

"Ha-ha. You bet. Half done already." Reggie smiled back at her.

"Well, we were going to grab a table and scroll through the karaoke options. Will see you a bit," Aaron said.

"Okay boys. Enjoy," Kimberly smiled back. She then walked over to another patron as her large breasts jiggled back and forth.

"Damnnnnn. Look at the Mammaquatia on her." Travis pointed out and looked over his shoulders. It was a fun word the three of them randomly found while doing research for a science project.

"Ha-ha. Mammaquatia (the bouncing of a woman's breasts when she walks, runs or exercises) I love the word so much." Reggie laughed and scanned the Michael Jackson song options in the karaoke binder.

Aaron approved with a beer chug. "I'm going to get me another beer. You pussies going to have another?"

"Yeah, go get us some beer, bitch!" Travis chalked said and took a quick glance at Kimberly serving a couple a plate of mushroom Swiss burgers. Reggie glanced at the score of the Brewers score on the small TV and then surveyed the array of artifacts in the tavern. He turned in his chair taking a drink of beer and stared at two eyes and a snake that were written in the hieroglyphics on the wall. The eyes beamed back at him and he started to cough violently from swallowing beer down the wrong pipe.

"Okay there, champ?" Travis grinned and finished off his beer.

"Yeah, yeah, those symbols over there give me the creeps. I wonder if they were trying to communicate with the dead or some shit," Reggie cleared his throat and wiped his face with a napkin.

"I don't believe in any of that shit man. I bet billions of people have died on earth since the beginning of time. If there was an afterlife, we'd be seeing ghosts daily and they'd be working at subways, carnivals, fast food joints and tollways to spare us our time. And hey, have you ever done an ancestry test before? I bet your entire family members are Mayans because you all have that fucking chicken scratch in your genes just like they did," Travis quipped and smash his beer can.

"Ha-ha, now that is fucking hilarious. What the hell is taking Aaron so long," Reggie roared with laugher smashing his hands on the table and they both glanced at Aaron at the bar.

"I'll take three shots of whiskey, please Ms. Kimberly," Aaron said with charm sitting at a bar stool watching the Brewers make a double play to end the inning

"Oh, you remember my name now there sweetie? Ha. What kind of whiskey are you looking there for Douglas?" she winked bank.

"Wait, wait what? Aaron questioned with a lift of his eyebrows.

"Ha-ha, I'm mutual friends with some of your brother's friends. I know everything." Kimberly laughed and grabbed a bottle of whiskey off the shelf.

"Don't worry, you guys are safe here. Just don't get too out of control. And hey! This first round of shots is on me if I can join you three for one."

"For sure!" Aaron preached back and lowered closer to Kimberly. "Thanks for having our back," he whispered and turned over to his friends to signal them over to the bar.

"So what did you get all of us, chump? I thought three beers was an easy order." Travis snickered and threw away his beer can while approaching the bar.

"Oh you know just some good old shots of Johnnie Walker Black Label. I got us another round of beers too" Aaron taunted giving a wink to Kimberly.

"Oooohhhh big spender!" Reggie stated in delight and passed the shots of whiskey to everyone.

"Time to make another toast there, champ," Reggie said staring at Travis.

"All right, will do. In all seriousness, this one is to you guys. Let's cherish these awesome moments for the rest of our lives. As dumb as it may sound, let's toast to this song playing now. Because I'll never forget this night, dudes. Let's party and keep boozing," Travis said in excitement as he raised his shot glass in the air to Eve 6's *Here's To The Night*. Reggie, Aaron and Kimberly also rose their shot glasses, clicked and downed the shot.

"Woooo! That one went down smoothly! Good cheers for real, man," Aaron told Travis and kindly nodded his head in approval. Travis was right on queue with his toast; as the song was playing in the background, everyone had euphoric goosebumps, blanketing their souls as they held onto each other's shoulders and sang to the song. They were inspired by the very moment and knew their friendship had blossomed to its fullest potential. If they could have it their way, the three of them would live on the same block and lounge in their backyards sipping on whiskey, listening to country, watching the wood crackle on a bonfire. Their wife and kids would be tucked snuggly in bed and they'd watch the sunrise simply enjoying an inseparable bond of gratitude.

"Can you believe that we'll hopefully be in college to play football in less than a year?" Aaron sipped on his beer and looked at the other two across the table with a serious face.

"Ya man, I mean it's crazy how so many people like Coach Edwards think we have officially hit rock bottom. I don't think so at all. We are just getting started boys," Reggie said and raised his beer can for another cheer. Travis chugged his beer and slammed it down.

"Champ all night suckers! But yes, I think in honor of this night we need to do some sort of sweet mission. Let's steal a street sign for our place in college or some shit. Perhaps a dead-end sign for you, Reg?" Travis asked and motioned for three more beers to Kimberly.

"Ha ha. Sounds sweet as shit. Where'd you get this crazy fucking idea?" Reggie asked and Kimberly walked over smiling with three beer cans on a tray. She opened all the beer cans and Aaron and Reggie exchanged glances waiting for Travis to speak up.

"Am I interrupting something? Maybe girl talk?" Kimberly said with a big smile as she put her hand on the table to try to join in the fun. Her nails were painted in dark red and she had a ring on one of her fingers. The three guys stared at Kimberly in shock—she looked amazing. They didn't say a word and were all a deer in headlights; they had just gotten a full view of how even more beautiful she looked outside of the bar area. She looked at all their faces as if it was a game of Russian Roulette, wondering who'd be the first one to break the silence and speak while cocooned in her provocative posture.

"Ha ha, you guys are funny." Kimberly softly walked away and took her phone out from her breasts to check her messages.

"When do the festivities begin?" Aaron shouted back quickly as she neared the bar. Aaron took a sip of his beer; she turned around and held up nine of her fingers signaling that the Kegaroke would begin at 9:00 PM. As Reggie, Aaron and Travis sat at the table watching the Brewers game and competing over who could drink the most beer, Travis briefed the other two of a sweet college party his cousin invited to the past summer. The house that hosted the party had stolen street signs, pictures of attractive woman in swimwear, Wisconsin sports memorabilia and several deer wall mounts. Travis described the house as a Shangri-La; a happy, earthly, mystical paradise in a utopian setting with no worries whatsoever. All three were very intrigued by the idea of having the same spectacular setup when they all moved together in college.

Travis was a great doodler; Reggie and Aaron convinced him to draw a sketch of a blueprint of their Shangri-La.

Travis pulled out a pen and a piece of paper from his back pocket. That's exactly how he went to his class: no backpack, textbooks, folders, binders, scratch and sniff markers, mechanical pencils, protractor or calculator—just a simple red pen and a blank piece of paper to doodle, make paper footballs or use as a cheat sheet for exams. He unfolded the paper and examined all the answers from his history exam earlier that morning. On the other side, there was a doodle of an attractive naked woman with big breasts with a word bubble above her stating "Double Ds, Wanna Touch?" with her hand pointed to her breasts. Aaron and Reggie slapped their fists on the table and howled in laughter. Travis smiled back and noticed he didn't have enough room to draw on the paper, so he folded it into a paper football. Aaron hosted his hands up to create a field goal post and Travis flicked it as hard as he could right into his face.

"It's good!" Reggie screamed holding his hands up high in the air. Aaron shook his head and laughed while rubbing his nose. Travis scanned the bar and noticed a beer coaster on the adjacent table. He took a sip of his beer and drew out a map of his proposed plan where all the street signs, the sports memorabilia, kegs, party posters and pictures of the attractive woman would go throughout the living room, bathroom and kitchen. Aaron and Reggie leaned over with fascination as they watched the artist at work. Aaron pointed at the dead-end sign and took a drink of his beer.

"I guarantee we'd get more chicks if we did that shit. I propose we get the sign in Reggie's neighborhood later tonight. Dead end, it is your property anyway, right?" Aaron suggested to Reggie and took a chug of beer.

Like knights at the round table, all three used their beer cans for a stamp of approval and discussed their plan of attack for later that evening with huge grins on their faces. As more beer was consumed and more shots were ordered, they were so hooked on that idea that their laughter ricocheted off their cans of beer, bar stools and into the patio filled with people smoking cigarettes and cigars.

"Alright, if we want to take care of this shit tonight, we should probably bounce shortly. Does your dad still have that huge saw in the garage, Aaron?" Reggie asked while still wiping tears from his eyes from all of the debaucheries.

"Yep. So again, like we all agreed on: I'll be the lookout. You two saw the sign down as quickly as possible and will carry it into the treehouse in my backyard. Let's get one more round and then head out," Aaron said and turned around to people watch. More and more patrons had come in. There were several groups of people hanging out together at different booths throughout the bar: a bachelorette party, a group of young professionals for a work outing, a man and woman that appeared to be on their first date, Charlie (the town drunk) and his drinking buddies, and another group of girls that appeared to be from their same high school.

"Holy fucking shit! I hadn't noticed how packed this place had gotten with all this banter. I don't know guys, but I think we may have to stay just a little bit longer," Travis said with a huge grin. "I know, I got Angela, but I can be the perfect wingman for you guys. Seems to be a lot of fish in the pond tonight," Travis said and turned around in his chair glancing around the scene. Aaron and Reggie looked at each other laughing and nodded.

"I can't believe Rebecca Swanson is here. Ha, that's good shit," Aaron said pointing in her direction. According to them, Rebecca was one of the most attractive girls at their school. Although she was popular, she was rumored to get around with all of the jocks. She was a shorter girl wavy blonde with highlights, blue crystal eyes, large breasts. Perfectly fit and had a contagious smile. Many of the students thought she was Marilyn Monroe's doppelgänger; she would often wear clothing that revealed her midriff and wore so much makeup that she looked like she was twenty-four when she was only eighteen. She did modeling from time to time and others believed she was also sleeping around with older men. Rebecca had walked over to the professional men who were at a work outing and went up to them with a confident posture as she sipped out of her Long Island seductively.

"I had a chance to hit that shit like a year ago," Travis shook his head in amazement at how stunning she was. "Damn, so many hot girls here tonight. What are you two pussies waiting for? Go get some ass! Tonight is our time to shine, boys. Let's rage. We are in control, baby!" Travis continued with that million-dollar smile he had. He regularly had his teeth whitened and was praised by many for having the "best smile" in the school, according to the yearbook senior superlatives. Aaron, on the other hand, won "most athletic" and Reggie had won "best sneakers."

"Ladies and gents, I'm Mikey Max and I will be your host for the evening. Tonight we have our ever so popular Thursday event, Kegaroke. Looks like we got a great crowd tonight so it should be a fun time. Remember the rules: any person or group has one chance to perform one song in the next hour. The best vote will receive a free keg party here for any Saturday that they choose. Again, I'd like to thank everyone for coming out tonight. If you have any questions, please come and see me. To the right of me are the big books of all the songs we have available. Good luck everyone and enjoy the show." Mikey was a taller black man wearing a nice polo shirt and dark blue jeans. He was in his thirties and had a bald head with a very thick beard. The crowd cheered and applauded as he introduced the first contestant onto the stage.

"What do you think you are doing?" Aaron asked as Reggie nonchalantly walked away from the table and walked over to the books with all the song options.

"You'll see," Reggie answered back with a smile as he drunkenly wobbled away. Aaron and Travis nodded their heads as they watched three girls dance around on stage to Backstreet Boy's *Bye Bye Bye*. Aaron whistled out a loud catcall and one of the girls returned the favor by giving him the bird. Reggie returned and glanced at Travis in shock pointing at Aaron; he roared in laughter as they high-fived each other.

"That was funny as shit," Reggie yelled over the music in the background. Reggie glanced at Aaron letting out a smile and tilted his head back and poured beer down into his mouth holding the can two feet over his head. The Karaoke song concluded and many began to applaud the performance. Aaron shrugged and covered his face as the three girls who just performed walked near him. All three of the women were a part of the bachelorette party. They were in their late twenties, wearing leather boots and matching pink shirts that said 'Bride Tribe.'

"So are you going to buy this girl a drink or what?" one of the girls said and put her boot on the table. The other two grabbed onto her shoulder to make sure she was balanced right and started laughing. The girl was the same that flipped Aaron off earlier. She wore glasses and had long dark hair down to her butt. She looked like a hot seductive math teacher and Aaron began to blush looking up at her while she rubbed her thighs. The bachelorette was drinking a margarita on the rocks and had big beautiful blue eyes, red hair, freckles and a crown on her head. The other one was a smaller girl supporting pigtails with jet black hair. She had a birthmark on the left side of her face and wore dark lipstick and a gothic necklace.

"Um, yes sure… what did you have in mind?" Aaron asked the girl as she was already motioning to the bartender to bring three shots of Jägermeister over to them. Kimberly brought over the shots of the thick, spicy, black licorice-flavored

German liqueur; the girls cheered, took the shots and slammed them on the table. One of them rested her hand on the back of Aaron's shoulder and whispered something in his ear. Travis and Reggie's nudged each other and covered their mouths trying to let out roars of laughter. The three girls turned away and blew kisses as the spurs of their boots clinked away. Seven other girls were cheering for their return, laughing and pointing at Aaron.

"Holy shit. What the fuck did she say, man?" Travis asked with his eyes beaming.

"Ha. That bitch just said 'thanks for the shot, kid.' That was kind of embarrassing but at the same time it was also very very arousing. I think I may have to check my boxers," Aaron replied.

"Ha ha, gross dude!" Reggie screamed and laughed hysterically. Travis held up his beer can and nodded his head in approval of what they all just encountered. They clicked beers and took a big swig to further enjoy the moment. Reggie flipped back his shaggy hair, put his hands on the back of his head and relaxed with his feet on another chair.

"Life is fucking perfect, boys. It's like we've already reached self-actualization of Maslow's Hierarchy of Needs or some shit…" Reggie looked around the bar to evaluate how hopping the bar had become. The all turned away from the TV and glanced over at Mikey Max who was walking back to the stage with a piece of paper in his hand.

"All right. Who's up next? Who's up next? We got a trio of dudes coming up next," Mikey announced as Reggie's eyes beamed in appreciation. "Hmmm. This should be quite interesting. Good choice of song too. Singing *Pour Some Sugar On Me* by Def Leppard. We got Reggie, Aaron and Travis."

As soon as Mikey announced it, Aaron and Travis glanced at each other in disbelief and turned to Reggie who greeted them only with the snarling, hideous sound of a hyena. Reggie convinced them singing on stage would capstone the evening in a big way. He immediately got up from his relaxed state and started coaxing the other two up onto the stage.

The crowd began to cheer them on, including the bachelorette girls. Reggie pointed back at their table with a huge grin on his face to acknowledge their cheers as Aaron and Travis selfishly sat in their chairs refusing to get on stage. The crowd started to hackle Aaron and Travis for not getting up, so Reggie went onto the stage by himself.

The song started blasting and Reggie sang the lyrics to the song with all the passion anyone could ask for. He showed his spin moves in between verses and screamed out to the crowd when the chorus came on to aid them to join in on the fun. "POUR SOME SUGAR ON ME!!!"

Everyone in the crowd raised their drinks and screamed at the top of their lungs. Instant global ear deterioration. Aaron and Travis were now both jealous of how Reggie was mesmerizing the audience and ran up onto the stage to join their friend. They all participated in singing the lyrics together and added their goofy dance moves to get the crowd to laugh more. Decibel levels were through the roof and no big bad wolf was going to huff and puff these three little piggies' house of entertainment down.

At this point, the bachelorette girls didn't want to miss out on the action. Kimberly stopped serving patrons to watch the crowd and let out a loud whistle of encouragement. The bachelorette girls marched on top of the stage and they coaxed Aaron to crowd surf. Without hesitation, Aaron free fell into the crowd and he was passed along the bar like a rag doll. The chorus came back and Travis started yelling profanities into the microphone. It had become so repulsive that Mikey finally turned the microphone off. The song ended and Reggie bowed to the crowd who responded with a standing ovation and non-stop laughter.

The DJ put on *It Was A Good Day* by Ice Cube for the intermission and the bachelorette girls danced like they had hula hoops around their waists. One of them went over to Aaron and suddenly took off his belt. Travis and Reggie, who were still on top of the stage, were in shock and could not believe what their musical performance had escalated into. Travis jumped off the stage and grabbed one side of Aaron's belt as Aaron held the other side. They held the belt in the air and encouraged the girls to participate in doing the limbo. Reggie proceeded to follow the girls and joined in on the fun. As everyone went through, Aaron and Travis made it more difficult by lowering the belt. The bouncer finally decided the debauchery had gone too far; he walked over with his chest out, cracked his knuckles and tugged on his long goatee looking down at the three guys.

"I'm going to have to ask you three to leave. We got a lot of complaints about the profanity and lewd behavior," he said glaring at the drunken three smiling back at him.

"No, they can stay," the girls begged the bouncer.

"Yeah, what's your fucking problem, douchebag? No one's bitching, your just jealous of all the fun we're having that you aren't." Aaron snapped back.

"Excuse me? That's it. Get the fuck out of here!" the bouncer screamed as he began to tug onto Aaron's shoulder. Aaron softly pushed him away and walked towards the door. Travis knew that their ship had finally sailed and quickly went to the bar to pay the tab of the additional shots they ordered. Reggie tried to get the girls' numbers, but the bouncer spun him around. Reggie yanked onto the bouncer's goatee as hard as he could and ran out the patio exit to join Aaron and the bouncer winced in pain. Travis witnessed as he waited for Kimberly to return his change. He waved his hand to keep it all and hid in the bathroom.

"You fucking pieces of shit! If I see you guys here again, I'm calling the cops. Stay the fuck away," the bouncer screamed as Aaron and Reggie ran into the cornfields that were overshadowed by the darkened moonlight.

"Ew, someone took a shit in the urinal. Who the fuck did this?" some patron, an older man dressed in camouflage, screamed as he walked into the men's bathroom. Travis was hiding in the stall and decided to make a run for it. He brushed by the older man who was plugging his nose. The man tried to grab him, but Travis escaped and passed the bouncer with a huge grin on his face. He caught up to the other two sitting on a very large tree log that had fallen over from a recent thunderstorm.

"Ha ha. That was fucking epic. This tree log is nothing! I left them a nice log of shit in their urinal," Travis yelled while coughing to catch his breath. Travis itched his short trimmed hair and they all busted out laughing.

"Looks like we made some friends this evening." Reggie quipped wiping sweat from his forehead that was oozing from his shaggy hair.

"We ain't done yet, boys; we got our mission to accomplish," Aaron delightfully replied while squinting his eyes from sweat that had dropped due to the adrenaline sonic boom they had all endured over the last hour. Aaron stood up from the log and pulled out his phone scanning for messages. "I don't think we can go back there to pick up the car until tomorrow morning," he added.

"Yeah, I think we may all be a little too wasted to drive that fucker home anyways. Call us a cab, Aaron. I'm not picking up any Uber drivers in the area." Reggie replied.

"Shit, these fucking mosquitos are bad. Yeah, let's get the hell out of here," Travis said as he swatted a mosquito off his neck. It was happy hour for the pesty tiny blood-sucking vampires and they wanted their two-for-one deal on his neck.

"You got another on your back," Aaron said and gave Travis a wicked smack on the back even though he didn't have one on. Reggie let out a chuckle.

"What the hell? You didn't have to give me a five star," Travis said.

"Had to make sure I killed the offspring too," Aaron laughed.

Aaron called a cab and was informed it'd arrive in ten minutes. The three of them wobbly walked a little further away from the bar to a Kwik Trip gas station to pick up energy drinks. They slurped on Red Bulls while reminiscing about how entertaining their evening had been, but yet realized their night was far from a climax. The cab driver arrived and they hopped into the Ford Crown Victorian. Aaron confirmed the address the driver repeated from his GPS. The other two looked at Aaron wondering why he selected a different address and he signaled for them to keep quiet with a finger on his lips.

CHAPTER 4

The cab driver was an older taller man from Russia. He was wearing a soccer t-shirt and chest hair was crawling out of his shirt. He was doused in an aftershave that was whopping a very pungent odor of musty Sandalwood. Aaron elbowed Reggie who was plugging his nose and rolled down the window. With his thick Russian accent, the driver asked how the evening was for the three boys. Silence. The aftershave was unbearable and they could hardly breathe. The driver turned to face the cold shoulder trio and tilted his head back laughing that he had been ignored. He turned down the radio (80's classic rock) as he neared the address Aaron had provided.

"Okay, you guys stay here quick, I got to run into the house to get some cash to pay this guy," Aaron lied as he opened up the door. He walked over to the front door and the driver shifted back to look at the other two staring at each other expecting the unexpected. Aaron pretended to open the front door with a pair of keys and then slowly turned back to the cab driver, flipped him off and bolted around the side of the house waving his hand in a violent motion to recruit Travis and Reggie from the backseat. They both immediately busted out laughing and frantically freed themselves from the car without saying a word; they sprinted to catch up to Aaron. The cab driver went berserk and raced out of his car like a speeding freight train with devil-infused pistons.

"Get the fuck back here, you punks! I'm calling the cops," he yelled as he was gaining distance behind Travis. Travis' shoes fell off as he was looking back at the driver. The other two were way up in front cheering Travis on to hurry up. Now shoeless, Travis had slipped on the grass. The cab driver grabbed and pinned him down using his arm like a crowbar over his neck.

"I got you now, you dumbass," the driver yelled as he pulled out his cell phone to call the cops. Travis gasped for air and begged for the driver to get off him, but he wouldn't budge. Aaron and Reggie started to tiptoe towards the scene to get a better look at the struggle and overheard the driver begin to report the incident to a dispatcher. Travis struggled violently to break free get away, but the cab driver pressed down on his neck harder. The driver glared a satisfying smile with missing teeth as Travis' face started to turn blue and started to explain the crime and The ditched cab fare was just about to put a bookmark on their mischievous escapades.

And then the unthinkable happened. The best escape tactic anyone could ever think of while drunkenly stupor was to get out of an aggravating conundrum. The driver set his phone down on the ground and screamed "What the fuckkkkk!?" as he began to feel warmth against his legs. Travis started to piss himself to try to prevent the tall, older Russian man from choking him any longer. The driver was in disbelief, slowly released Travis from his grip and screamed "Nu vse, tebe pizda!" meaning 'that's it, you're a dead man." Travis began to violently cough gasping for air and the dispatcher became concerned about a potential life or death situation asking the driver to repeat himself. Travis finally noticed he was free and ran towards his feet grabbing onto his neck in agony. The Russian was looking back and forth at Travis with his shirt, pants and hands in urine. He hung up the phone on the dispatcher and screamed more Russian vulgarities. As he violently walked past to his car, he noticed Travis' missing sneakers. He flashed his missing teeth glaring smile and tried the pair of Nike Air Zooms on. Perfect fit: the cab fare was covered with a generous tip after all.

"In all of this madness, this chaos, this pandemonium... I just remembered we still have our Homecoming football game tomorrow," Reggie stated in delight as he pulled out his phone to look at the time. "11 PM. Do you think we should wait until tomorrow to do this mission? I mean Christ, Travis... you pissed yourself to prevent us from getting a fine. You also lost your brand new pair of sneakers.

"Fuck it, you have like thirty pairs in your closet. He can borrow one of your pairs for a little while. The night ain't over yet. Travis's brilliant idea of sign sealing will not surrender. It's happening tonight," Aaron fired back, shook his head at Reggie and continued to look up and down at the urine soiling on Travis' pants, discolored neck and dirty socks. Travis shrugged and combed his nicely trimmed hair under the distant moonlight. Dogs began to bark violently back at each other and they decided that it was time to get a move on. They crept along the roadside to get back to Aaron's house as they watched for cars. Whenever a car passed, they would duck down near the ditch to ensure the Russian cab driver or police weren't out looking for them.

They finally approached Aaron's house and noticed the light was still on in the family room. "Shit, my dad must be up waiting up for me. One second, I got an idea," Aaron said and pulled out his phone. He dialed his parents' house and watched the window from across the street to see his dad walk towards the phone.

"Hello?" Aaron's dad replied.

"Yo dad, it's Aaron," Aaron answered back.

"Where in the hell are you? It's 11 PM." He shouted back.

"I'm sleeping out in the treehouse tonight with the guys. We've been here for the past few hours, but I just woke up noticing you had the light on," Aaron fibbed glancing over at Travis and Reggie who looked concerned.

"Fine. Just go back to bed now, will ya? Big game tomorrow for you guys," he scolded.

"Yeah, yeah, yeah I know. We were actually prep talking about the game. Good night, Dad," Aaron said with a serious tone to keep his dad from going irate. Reggie and Travis covered their mouths as they began to violently snicker. Aaron's dad hung up the phone without saying anything else and Aaron gave a high-five to Reggie and Travis for his superb idea. Aaron was brilliant when it came to lying to his parents; they always knew he was up to no good but he barely got in trouble with the police, so the fibs he architected out from under his ass always came in handy. They walked a few blocks away to Travis' house who lived in the same neighborhood as Aaron.

"Genius. 110 percent fucking genius," Travis exclaimed as they walked through the side door of his parents' garage. Aaron flipped on the lights and opened the fridge. He saw some leftover butternut squash ravioli and dipped his hands in it to cup into his mouth. He then licked the sauce off his fingers and Travis and Reggie shook their heads laughing. They searched around the garage for the big saw they were going to use to chop down the dead-end sign. Reggie spotted one in the back corner of the garage and carefully took it down from the clamps it was placed on. Travis snatched the saw from Reggie and they crept outside. Aaron slowly closed the door behind him and off they went into the darkness for the next adventure of the evening.

Travis steadily held the saw close to his side as the other two followed close behind. They played frogger through backyards attempting to avoid sensor lights and let out silent laughter knowing another dosage of adrenaline was about to kick in. They were about twenty feet from the dead-end sign when they saw a white Ford Taurus approaching them at a fast speed. The boys quickly jumped into the bushes and crept down watching the car pass. The car stopped in the middle of the road and began to go in reverse back towards them. When it finally stopped just six feet from them, it was almost as if they were rapidly approaching six feet under themselves. No last meal opportunity. Already injected with embalming chemicals. Obituaries printed. Eulogies read. Parents weeping and saying their prayers. The coffin for their very own lives was being lowered by the pallbearer second by second as this car sat and stared in the middle of the street drafting their death warrants.

An older man with a scruffy beard, long gray hair tied into a ponytail got out of his car and walked around the side of his vehicle. He walked in a drunken manner and muttered things to himself as he got closer to the ditch where the boys were standing. He was wearing a thick brown dirty coat that was buttoned up. He took off his orange hunting hat, scratched his head and looked around the area. "Almost had me some free fucking deer," he exclaimed pulling a flask out of his pocket and took a large swig. He put the flask back into his pocket, scratched his large thick eyebrows and stumbled back to his car to slowly drive down the street. The man was Charlie, the town drunk who was coming back home from the bar they were all at earlier. He had almost witnessed them in the act of a crime. However, they too had just witnessed him commit a felony of driving drunk, but they had no desire to report that incident, of course; it would interrupt the rest of their evening."Good ol' Charlie," Travis sighed and patted the dirt off his jeans as he stood back up and took a long look down the endless road.

"Yeah, I didn't know he drove around drunk like that too. That guy is one fucking weird dude. Thinking that we were deer?" Reggie laughed and twirled his fingers around his long shaggy hair.

"All right, the coast is clear for now. Let's do this shit," Aaron ordered as he motioned towards the dead-end sign. As they discussed at the bar, Aaron was to be the watchdog while the other retrieved the sign. Reggie and Travis quickly ran across the street and began sawing away at the pole in a frantic fashion. They would often stop working and look back at Aaron doing the surveillance—he would return the favor by holding up an okay sign that it was still safe. After ten minutes, they successfully had taken down the sign and the three of them aided in hoisting it like it was the Stanley Cup running down the side of the road like they were in a championship parade. They screamed in excitement and bolted to Aaron's treehouse. Aaron's parents' house no longer had lights on so the coast seemed to be clear.

Ruff! Ruff! Ruff! Aaron's dog, Teddy, began to bark loudly from the window. Aaron looked back at his dog in distress and began hollering at Reggie and Travis to get the sign inside the treehouse immediately. Reggie desperately tried to open the lock with the key as sweat dripped down his face. Travis silently scolded him for being so slow. Pitch black morphed into a glistening evil bright light.

"Oh fuck," Aaron keeping watch muttered as Reggie finally got the lock to pry open. They tossed the dead-end sign and quickly hid in the treehouse and peaked out a crevice and heard his mom opening the door to let Teddy out. Teddy was sniffing around in the grass and Aaron's mom stood outside in a bathrobe gazing at the stars. They accidentally stepped on yard tools that made Teddy's ears pucker up. Teddy pounced downhill towards the treehouse and started to scratch at the ladder to get inside. As autumnal equinox neared, the stars twinkled in synchrony to the September Full Corn Moon, fallen leaves swirled around in circles to a soft brisk breeze and a pack of coyotes howled suggesting a hunt for a bedtime snack. Alarmed, Aaron's mom coaxed Teddy back inside with a Purina Beggin' Strip.

"That was a close one," Travis stated as he crawled over to the sleeping bags hanging onto the wall of the treehouse. He passed them out to the other two and Aaron continued to look out the window to make sure that they were finally safe. His mom and Teddy finally entered back inside and Aaron turned around and yelled. "We are fucking badass brothers," and shined the flashlight on the dead-end sign laying on the ground in the center between the three of them.

"True that, true that," Reggie said and started to make himself comfortable in the sleeping bag. "I think we should get some shut-eye," he added.

"Ha, yes this was seriously the most memorable night of our lives," Travis beamed flashing his shiny white teeth batting away a cobweb near his face.

"Hey, like you said, Travis… This was the most memorable night of our lives. And where we ended up tonight is something we'll never forget. Let's make a pact. Let's say if we don't end up going to the same college together or one of us ever dies before we make it to the real world, we demolish this treehouse as a memory?" Aaron asked the other two.

It'd be a very somber day to imagine the treehouse going down, yelling timber. Inside, there were many of Aaron's prized possessions from his childhood including yo-yo's, baseball cards, board games, bouncy balls, cereal box toys, beanie babies and comic books. His dad also was a big hoarder and kept old yard tools that barely worked inside; their mom often complained and begged them both to do a yard sale, but they wouldn't budge. On the walls, Aaron also tapped some of

Travis's drawings; his favorite was one of the *Teenage Mutant Ninja Turtles* lounging inside an aquarium while they snacked on a Chicago deep-dish pizza and watched the Green Bay Packers on a television.

The three of them also spent an entire summer building it with Aaron's older brother, Tyler. Portions of it had already been completed between Tyler and Aaron's father, but they never finished and Tyler jumped at the opportunity to help when he found his younger brother and his buddies wanted to master Frank Llyod Wright's craft for summer and finish building the treehouse. The three of them will always remember Tyler hammering away at a nail as he delegated tasks; their lunch breaks that involved dancing to the *Macarena* song on the radio, chugging gallons of raspberry lemonade and fighting over seconds of Caprese grilled cheese sandwiches on delicious sourdough bread.

"It's your treehouse," Reggie and Travis both answered together.

"No we all put work into it. It's ours. This thing goes down if we don't all make it to the top together. Including scholarships," Aaron put his hand in the middle of them. Reggie and Travis sat up and crawled on the squeaking floor moving closer to Aaron. They all put their hands together to form the pact. They were all excited and agreed to go to bed realizing that tomorrow night's game was the next chapter in their lives to continue to rise to the top of Maslow's Hierarchy of Needs--self-actualization.

CHAPTER 5

It was the second hour at school the next morning and Aaron was staring at himself in the mirror. He brushed chocolate long john donut crumbs off his goatee, glanced devilishly at his bloodshot eyes and wiped off the eye boogers. He let out a roaring yawn and went over to the urinal. After finishing doing his business, he walked to the sink to scrub his hands.

"Blahhhhhhhhhh!" Someone had just unleashed a projectile vomit in a stall near him. Aaron was startled; he turned around while creeping towards the stall door. He peaked down below and saw feet with only socks facing the toilet seat and throwing up sounds.

"This is ridiculous," the voice said in a high-pitched moan. Aaron noticed that it was Travis and crept back towards the bathroom sink with a slight smirk on his face. He began ripping off paper towels and soaking them with soap and water. He had about fifteen rounds of soapy paper balls for ammo and steadily walked back towards the stall carrying them in both his palms gently.

He opened up the adjacent door next to Travis—stood on top of the toilet seat and hunched over the edge and watched him shaking violently back and forth as he unleashed another sequence of vomit. Laughing violently, Aaron began to throw the wet soapy paper towels at Travis one by one. Travis sheepishly turned around and tried to bat them away with the back of his hand. Soap dripped into his bloodshot eyes from the paper towels. He let out a wince and threw up again and some of it plopped on the ground. Leftovers anyone? Butternut squash ravioli from last night's supper was for the taking. Travis let out another groan and put his hand on his chest. A sharp pain of heartburn struck him like a bat of hell and he started to dry heave. Travis leaned over on his side, put his hand on his hot steaming forehead and stared up at the ceiling like he was dead.

"Wake up dude, Coach Edwards can't see us like this. He will flip shit," Aaron said and coughed from the pleasure of harassing his vulnerable friend.

"Dude, I feel like complete shit. Go away. I'm serious," Travis groaned back. *Rinnngggggggggg! T*he bell alarmed the students passing period was over.

"Dude, you can't play tonight if you miss any classes. I'll try to cover you for as long as I can but you gotta make it to English," Aaron said and let out another yawn. Aaron walked out of the bathroom and saw Reggie sitting at the back table where they always sat during second hour. Aaron explained to Reggie what he had witnessed and Reggie laughed chirping back that he made himself throw up this morning, ate a huge breakfast his mom had made him and took a large dosage of Tylenol. According to him, he now felt one hundred and ten percent.

Travis opened the classroom—he wiped remains of puke from his face. Aaron and Reggie both covered their faces to avoid a squeal and turned back to the teacher who was talking about an exam that was going to take place next week. Travis sat down next to them both, put his hoodie on and rested his head between his two arms on the table. They both stared at him—Reggie was about to give Travis a wet willy but Aaron decided to hold him back; he had already unleashed some pain to him in the bathroom. Reggie reluctantly agreed and scrolled through social media on his phone.

As class went on, some of the other students whispered over to Aaron about what they heard from last night's practice. He nodded back beaming a smile to acknowledge he knocked former Navy Seal, Coach Edwards to the ground. Aaron didn't seem too pleased about all his classmates knowing about the incident. In the back of his mind, he knew he had to be more disciplined in school and extracurricular activities. Aaron turned over to Travis who was drooling a dream of dismay and smiled while opening up his textbook to engage in the review the English teacher was covering.

***

It was finally nearing the end of the ninth hour when Aaron stared at the clock tapping away at the floor—his feet hoping that his foot would help jockey the end of class to the finish line. He was in Mrs. Gleason's class, the teacher that was failing him in science and who saw him drink a beer while driving home from practice. Aaron turned his head away from the documentary on the impact of climate change, rested his hand on his chin and stared out the window where he could see the football field. The place of glory. The place of history. He still had a slight hangover. Misery. Tonight would be the biggest game of his life.

A crew was prepping the field, and even though he was stuck inside a musty-smelling classroom filled with other teenagers he could embrace the aroma of the oncoming breathtaking scent of autumn. He could feel the freshly painted lines on the lush green football field, envision the pigskin soaring through the air towards him, hear the crowd erupting in excitement and the referees blowing their whistles signaling a touchdown, and his coach yelling to congratulate him on a spectacular one-handed catch.

Ringggggg! The last bell rang and Aaron awoke from his dazed and confused state of dreaming about football. He packed up his bag and let out a sigh—the weekend was finally here. Not only was it hours before game-time, but some festivities would conclude the game.

Aaron walked out of the classroom door and Mrs. Gleason shut the door abruptly in front of him. Stunned, Aaron dropped his book bag and backpedaled by knocking into a table behind him that caused pieces of human anatomy set to fall over. Mrs. Gleason had frizzy brunette hair and wore glasses, and she often wore big earrings and headbands. She was very attractive but didn't have the playful attitude you'd expect. She was a hard worker and always got what she wanted. She would always dress more professionally than the rest of her colleagues, and consistently had a water bottle in her hand.

"Aaron, we need to talk," she said as she sipped out of her bottle of water. Aaron bent over to pick up the pieces and noticed he held onto the heart that now had a dent in it. His own heart duplicated the pain of the anatomy one as it was beating like a ticking time bomb with seconds to erupt. "Here, Take a seat. Don't worry about that mess, I'll take care of it. I know you have your big game tonight but this won't take long."

"Look Mrs. Gleason, I'm really sorry about yesterday. I know it was a big mistake not to pull over for you and talk then." Aaron looked down at the ground like a guilty whimpering puppy who had just pissed all over a brand new living room carpet.

"Yeah, that was pretty low of you, Aaron. It upsets me and I am still ashamed of you drinking a beer while driving. I should follow my responsibilities and advise the administration of this incident. But, I have given it some thought and decided to cut you a break. Still, the fact that you did that is concerning. Who are you trying to impress? And do you have an alcohol problem?" She asked back showing a concerned frown of disappointment.

"No, no, no it was just me being stupid!" Aaron pleaded back. "You won't see me do it ever again. I swear to you."

"Okay, I strongly believe in giving people a second chance to, but you really need to get your act together before you wind up making a mistake you'll never regret. I know you don't want to hear me lecture you. You're thinking I do that every ninth hour so this is too much, right? I know you're a good kid,

Aaron, I really do. It just wouldn't be right for me to not step in and try to prevent some of your actions if I'm seeing it firsthand. You know, if I brought this up to Principal Swanson, your future wouldn't be looking so sharp. One more chance, that's it!"

"I don't really know what to say, but I'm sorry. I'm not doing too hot in this class but trust me I'll be ready for the exam this coming Monday," Aaron replied noticing Travis and Reggie with concerned looks out the window with his peripheral vision.

"I would really appreciate it if you did. Your generation must pay attention to climatology because our planet's future really depends on it. One other favor I ask of is—" Mrs. Gleason paused and took another sip from her water bottle.

"Yeah?" Aaron asked while beaming his eyes towards Mrs. Gleason. Mrs. Gleason took one more drink of her water and stared devilishly into Aaron's eyes and moved closer to him.

"Please don't fuck with my house during your traditional chaos on faculty's property next week. We just did some remodeling and beautiful landscaping and it'd be a damn shame to have to hunt down punk kids to press charges. I know my address is not listed, but I know what all of you guys are capable of doing, especially these days," she said.

"Understood. I will personally make sure your house is not targeted." Aaron nodded his head and put on his backpack. He opened the door handle, stared back towards her direction noticing she had discovered the heart with the dent. He thought *she probably wants to rip my own heart out now, but I'm so thankful she has a heart of gold.*

Aaron knew that this particular incident was not going to prevent him from participating in "Fuck the Faculty Week." It was a ritual that began in the early 2000s as practical pranks leading to more serious crimes such as vandalism. This particular week generally followed Homecoming week, but would sometimes be spontaneously rescheduled a week before to keep the teachers on their toes. As more and more students got charges for their actions, the number of incidents had dropped, but it was now a transition back to a more practical prank state. School administration threatened two weeks of school suspension and a five-game suspension for any sport the student was participating in. Five games were half the football season; a scholarship offer would be shred in half if caught.

***

"Big game tonight, fellas. Ready to party like a fucking rock star at my dad's crib after the game? We are going to tear it up tonight with booze, bitches, billiards, ball, burgers, brats, and bonfire. Fuck yeah!" Bruce, who played the center position for the football team, slammed his locker in thrill. Naughty adult and sports cars pictures were pinned all over his locker. He was overweight and stood stocky at about 5'9". He could be classified as a hick—he always wore a flannel buttoned-down shirt, a cowboy hat and a thick non-groomed beard. He e was one of the most popular kids at school for his aggressive partying antics and owning a Chevy Silverado with a very impressive upgraded exhaust system. After the football season was over, he would do his legendary routine: donuts on the football field. He was one of the captains of the football team and had started as a center since freshman year.

His dad's cabin was a hidden gem in a wooded adjacent to the Cedar Creek. It had a large backyard that could host an array of entertainment with a sand volleyball court, outdoor basketball court, pool, hot tub, marble stone bar and gigantic fire pit. His parents had a family-owned mechanic shop that had been in business for over a century. Bruce would throw parties often; his parents would visit his grandmother up North in Door County who was suffering from Alzheimer's. Bruce would go with them on occasion to show his sympathy but preferred to stay back to maintain his status as a senior ruling the hallways at Cedar Creek High School.

"Yeah… fuck yeah… man of course I will be there," Aaron replied sitting next to Reggie and Travis in the locker room. Bruce gave them all a fist pump and walked away to his locker. Tick tock, tick tock, tick tock, the clock slowly made its circles as the three of them ate peanut butter and banana pregame fuel sandwiches and blasted heavy metal to get pumped for Friday Night Lights.

"First play is a touchdown to you, Aaron," Travis exclaimed wiping crumbs off his face and coming back his hair. "No matter what Coach E calls, I'm bombing an eighty-yard bomb right to you. Let's show these scouts what we're made of. Let's show Edgewater that they don't deserve to be in our conference or on our field," he added while jump shooting a lunch bag into the garbage.

"Hell yeah, dude," Aaron screamed in pleasure as he sipped down a Fruit Punch Gatorade. "I still can't believe how shitty you were this morning. That was funny as hell," Aaron laughed and stared at Travis sporting his nicely whitened teeth with a grin.

"Ha-ha, yeah I didn't think you were going to make it through the day," Reggie responded while he began untying his gym shoes.

"Yeah, it had gotten so bad that I had to go into the nurse's office and say that I had a massive migraine," Travis replied while motioning quotation marks with his hands for the migraine—his massive hangover. "Luckily they excused it, otherwise I may have not been able to play. It also sucked walking around the halls just in socks all day too. I miss my Nike Air Zooms so much There was no way I was wearing my cleats all day." Reggie handed him an extra pair of shoes from his locker and Travis returned a thankful high-five for the generosity. Coach Edwards walked in with his clipboard and rubbed his eyes as if he had just woken up from a nap. He tipped his baseball cap to the three boys walked by whistling without saying a word. Aaron gave his coach a head nod.

"What are you, his little bitch now?" Reggie muttered under his breath while smirking at Aaron. Aaron slowly turned around on the bench and responded by giving Reggie a light Charley horse on his knee.

"Try running the ball with that pain now," Aaron replied back as Reggie let out a small shriek of pain. Aaron walked over to the mirror and applied paint under his eyes as he stared at Reggie and Aaron mocking the "new bonding" he now had with the coach. Aaron shook his head and smiled as he chewed his gum and flexed his biceps in the mirror. He knew that there wasn't really a chance to defend himself; he realized that at this point it would be best to respect his coach. If he didn't obey, he could potentially lose his starting job or any future scholarship opportunities. Aaron felt he had the best shot of getting a scholarship to play collegiate football out of all three—it was best to keep his mouth shut while on the field for the rest of the season. He didn't care what others thought of that notion; playing at Camp Randall Stadium on Saturdays in front of an electric Wisconsin Badger crowd was a constant daydream DeJa'Vu delight.

CHAPTER 6

It was now 7:00 PM and the entire team was suited up, jumping up and down screaming, shoving each other to amp themselves up while they were waiting to be announced by the MC. Homecoming had arrived and protecting their nest from the challenging crusaders was the only objective. No time for laying rotten eggs; only Silver Eagles eggs that promised to hatch a triumphant victory later this evening.

"Let's take care of fucking business boys. Soar! Soar! Soar!" Bruce bellowed at the top of his lungs and rapidly drummed his hands on his helmet; the team responded as an orchestra following Bruce, their conductor to mirror his actions. Adrenaline had begun to rapidly jolt through the young man's bloodstreams. Coach Edwards smiled back in approval and appreciation; it gave him confidence his team was ready to succeed and give one hundred percent effort on the field. It was something the team always did on game day—he just wanted more of it during team practice.

"And nowwwwwwwwwww! Get everyone on your feet! Here comes your Cedar Creek Silver Eagles!" the MC screamed into the PA system. The fans went into a fiery anticipation as the team exploded out of the tunnel waving their arms up to get the crowd roaring and soaring. The crowd flapped their wings to honor the team's nickname and the student band blasted the school theme music. Parents, students, faculty and former alumni cheered and held out signs of encouragement. Some fellow students—already intoxicated— screamed vulgarities at the opposing rival team that was with stretch exercises across the field. The drunken obscenities were met by parents scolding their behavior. The students began to shake their keys in their fists and yell out student chants accompanied by the cheerleaders. Then, the earthquake—it involved the student section rocking back and forth, a tradition that started in the parking lots while in their cars. Every single home game felt as if a red carpet had been laid out for the team; they ran out while everyone partied like wild animals.

The team was on top of the world; they were blanketed with warmth and respect for the entire community. No one could stop the unit, and the pistons of their runaway freight train were going maximum overdrive with no brake pads in sight. As the team locked arms and shoulders together staring down enemy territory, it felt as if the end zone was the pot of gold fulfilling all accomplishments they could ever hope for. They were embracing the moment as much as they could—it was Homecoming night against one of their most hated cross- town rivals for the past century. The athletic directors headlined the teams on either opening prep football night or homecoming every year to keep ongoing friendly wagers thriving about the rivalry. Both of the teams were currently tied in the conference and were competing for first place.

"I know that yesterday was a bit of a bullshit day, men, but I'm here to win. I get chills just thinking about us hosting a state trophy. I know we as a unit have the championship caliber to do so. So that's why I lose my temper and patience with you guys. I know you guys want this shit as much as me. Let's take first place and show the state, no let's show the world what we're made of," Coach Edwards screamed with a raspy voice. The team hollered back at their Coach's prep speech and all put their hands together. "LET'S GO EAGLES!"

As Travis always did before a game, he turned to the crowd and pointed out to his girlfriend Angela and pretended to throw a football at her. Angela would always pretend to catch it and her girlfriends would let out a collective "Ooooooooooooohhhhhh" as all of Travis' teammates gave him shit for it. They all respected the hell out of him for doing it—he had one of the most attractive girlfriends in the entire school.

It was game time and the team was getting ready for kickoff. Aaron was set to receive and he pointed to the sky calling for a touchdown on the return. Everyone had questioned Aaron's decision to play wide receiver; he could've easily been a top-tier quarterback in the state. But he knew he would out-beat Travis for that position. Travis really wanted it and Aaron wanted every one of his friends to be happy. Aaron was one of the best athletes in the state and he could excel in any position he played at. Out of the three, he was the most respected for being so loyal and selfless.

Travis, who was set to block for Aaron, gave him a head nod letting him know he was going to do whatever it took to set him up for a touchdown. Aaron had already converted on three kickoff returns for touchdowns that season—pretty impressive. Recruiters were all over in the stands it was an important night and Aaron had to continue to build his relationship with Coach Edwards after their talk.

"Let's GOOOOO!" Bruce shouted using his hands to project his voice as the ball sailed through the air. Goosebumps of euphoria dripped out of Aaron's pores; he caught the ball and ran full sprint towards the goal line. Travis made a huge block on two players and Aaron juked a defender. Aaron was about to get tackled in the sidelines when Bruce came in with another successful block. The crowd was screaming and Coach Edwards was running down the sidelines jumping in delight.

Aaron broke three more tackles with a stiff arm, a spin move and a hurdle, then reached the end zone and kneeled down to celebrate. His teammates immediately shoved him over showing their appreciation. He just put an immediate dagger into the Edgewater Crusaders' heart.

"That a baby! That a baby!"Coach Edwards echoed as Aaron ran back to him on the sidelines. Coach Edwards gave him a fist pump with a jubilant smile. Coach Edwards was so proud he immediately thought a fist pump was not enough. He walked back to Aaron who was about to grab a cup of water and hugged him. Aaron was stunned at first, but hugged back. Travis and Reggie looked at each other in disbelief, and then looked back at Aaron and Coach Edwards shaking each other with explosive enthusiasm.

"What the hell is going on?" Aaron's father Austin asked while returning to Donna as he threw popcorn into his mouth. Donna shrugged and a tear dropped down her cheek as Aaron walked away from his coach with his helmet in hand heading to the bench to watch the next play.

***

Heading into the fourth quarter, the Silver Eagles were down by four points. They had lost their lead due to an interception Travis threw while under pressure from their menacing defense. Coach Edwards reamed out Travis violently for his decision-making and wanted Aaron to come in as quarterback, but he refused. "Travis will make up for it." Travis was a bit teary-eyed and emotional, and thanked Aaron for the support.

There were only twenty-five seconds left in the game with the ball in possession of the Silver Eagles on the thirty-five-yard line. The team went into the huddle and Travis was about to call a play that was directed by the coach. Aaron looked back up at Travis; then his coach and belted out, "Nuh uh, fuck that!"

The team looked over to him in shock—he was going against the coach's call. "We don't have enough time to fuck around and do quick plays. Let's go for the home run right now. Remember that play I drew up a few weeks ago when we were in the treehouse?" The majority of the team was baffled; they had no idea what play he was referring to.

"Fuck ya, I do," Reggie exclaimed nodding his head. "Let's do it." Aaron quickly explained the play to the team. It was essentially a Flea Flicker where Reggie would pitch the ball back to Travis and then launch it out to Aaron on a fly route who would initially hide behind Bruce at the beginning of the play. The team hurried to the line and Travis called "hut" and made the pitch to Reggie. Coach Edwards immediately threw his clipboard and looked at his assistant coaches as if they had to do something with the play call; they were just in shock as he was.

Travis received the ball back from Reggie and launched a perfect pass to Aaron who caught it at the twenty yard line. There were eight seconds left and the team was yelling at him to get out of bounds. Aaron kept going at high stride; a defender gained on him and started pulling him down, but he picked up his speed and dragged the defender until he fell off. Aaron was about to reach the goal line; he faced one more defender and struck him with an Adrian Peterson-like stiff arm. Then, he fell into the end zone exhausted. The crowd was roaring and Coach Edwards fell to the ground due to what he just witnessed. The team stampeded onto the field and toppled onto Aaron like he was an unclaimed winning lottery ticket. Tinnitus was pulsating throughout Aaron's eardrums and he was certain they'd gush with a lava flow of blood soon enough.

"Ha, hey fuckers, get off him so he can breathe!" Bruce shouted and helped Aaron to his feet. Aaron took off his helmet, covered his ears from the debilitated ringing and beamed his hazel eyes in glory. The Crusaders sat watching the

Silver Eagles fan base participate in "the earthquake" as *Fly Like an Eagle* by Steve Miller Band blasted over the loud speakers. It got so extreme that fans almost fell off the bleachers that the faculty had to run to control the earthquake and help lower the Richter scale of the student section. The aftershocks were inevitable.

"Can you believe what just happened? That was fucking amazing! That was fucking incredible!" Austin shrieked with his hands on top of his head; he noticed his mom in the stands shush him to control his foul language. Aaron reached the sidelines and Coach Edwards doused him with the Gatorade cooler. Coach Edwards had been shunned for wasting the Gatorade cooler earlier in the week in the blistering heat at practice; but today it wasn't wasteful. It was peaceful, a moment of gratifying bliss that couldn't be replicated. Coach Edwards handed Aaron the game ball as he gave a brief congratulatory. It had been an emotional rollercoaster in the past twenty-four hours and it couldn't have been a better ending.

"Look who is getting laid tonight, boyssss." Bruce giggled as he pulled two condoms from his locker. The entire team chuckled and one teammate, Nelson, screamed, "Ya, maybe if

Rebecca Swanson is there, then you actually have a chance."
He laughed.

"Looks like Nelson is no longer invited, you little pussy
bitch!" Bruce joked as he combed his long curly hair and put
deodorant on. Bruce was of Mexican descent and was
recognized as the main class clown. Falling through tables and
reciting lines from *Tommy Boy* and *Black Sheep* was one of his
pastimes because he idolized the late Chris Farley. Aaron,
Travis and Reggie approached Bruce at his locker and got the
lowdown of what the festivities were going to be tonight.
Ingredients for an epic bloodbath of excitement were in the
blender ready to be mixed with alcohol, drugs, sex, loud music
and loads of laughter.

CHAPTER 7

"Chug Chug Chug!" the entire party chanted as Bruce did a triple beer bong—a freshman held it at the top of the rooftop. Bruce high-fived his teammates.

"That was fucking awesome! Do it again! Do it again!" a little scrawny freshman with glasses shouted from the top of the roof.

"Shut the fuck up, you pussy freshman. Get the fuck down here and hit this bowl, bitch." Bruce laughed and wiped beer off his face. The freshman named Peter was a class nerd but was often invited to parties; his senior brother Nelson was on the football team. Nelson had curly hair and freckles and was one of the other receivers for the team. He was popular but was often picked on for also being very skinny and was generally the butt end of jokes.

"Stay up there, Peter, don't come down!" Nelson warned his brother who started to climb down a ladder.

"Are you fucking kidding me, twig? Dude, chill out, it's just one rip. He will be fine," Bruce shouted back and tried to coax Peter from coming down the ladder. "Dude, my mom will fucking kill me if she knows he smoked weed," Nelson winced back scratching his arms.

"Itching because you are a scared pussy ass bitch? Haha. Fine, whatever. I'll make him smoke it when you aren't looking." Bruce laughed and blew the smoke into Nelson's face. Nelson stood there and took the heat without saying a word. "Catch, it's the one thing your good at." Bruce sighed as he tossed Nelson to bowl for him to take a hit. Other partygoers snickered and walked into the house as Nelson looked up to his brother still on the roof—it was an obstacle the two of them faced together on a daily basis. They tried so hard to fit in. Nelson took a hit of the weed and walked into the house to join the party. Peter briefly took his glasses off and wiped tears from his eyes and slowly climbed down to join the fun.

"Chick Pillow fight!" Travis yelled and pointed over to the living room where three attractive girls were spraying each other down with whipped cream and hitting each other with fluffy pillows. One of them was Rebecca Swanson, who the three boys had seen at The Lucid Owl the previous evening. Furthermore, she was the daughter of the principal and felt she had to act in inappropriate activities so she wasn't shunned for being the daughter of the high-school administration.

"Woooooooo!" Rebecca shouted, shook up the whipped cream, sprayed it around her cleavage and took a pillow swing at her friends Molly and Kaitlin.

"This is fucking awesome!" Travis screamed at the top of his lungs. He then covered his mouth and laughed looking at Angela, his girlfriend, who was shaking her head as she leaned up against the wall chatting with some of her friends.

"Such a douchebag he can be sometimes, but I love the shit out of that fucker." Angela smiled back at Travis who was passing around beers to buddies.

Peter was standing in the corner by himself sipping out on a red solo cup watching the party with a slight smile. Across the room, Bruce motioned a "shh" signal to a few other football players and tiptoed behind Peter with a huge bong with large breasts sticking out of it. He tapped Peter on the shoulder and forced him to take a huge rip. Peter took a ten-second rip, coughed violently and walked over to the couch like a zombie to plant face first onto the couch. Bruce let out a hollow to the moon and several people in the room crackled. Nelson turned around to see his now dazed and confused brother passed out on the couch and shook his head in disappointment in Bruce. Bruce snickered and flipped him off.

The party went on for another forty-five minutes with total destruction of the house: younger freshmen started to puke in the upstairs' bathtub after being hazed to take several shots from Bruce. The music was blaring and Rebecca was making out with a sophomore named Lorenzo on the couch. Lorenzo was a tall foreign exchange student from Italy with spiked hair and a muscular tone. All the girls were attracted to his accent and they loved he would bring in home-cooked pizzas to the school for the ladies. The seniors nicknamed him Luigi and would steal slices of the za whenever they had a chance.

Lorenzo decided he had already gotten to second base and that it was time to steal for third and caressed Rebecca's breasts. Immediately her phone started ringing but she ignored it. It was her father. He kept calling but all she was interested in *was having the moon hit her eyes like a big pizza* pie by swapping tongue phlegm. That's amore! Nevertheless, she then let out a huge sigh and read a text message that her father sent to her.

"Hey! Don't IGNORE ME! You better not be at Bruce Hernandez's party. Got some phone calls from parents and the cops are heading that way now. Call me back ASAP!"

"What's wrong? Put your phone away," Lorenzo begged as he started to unzip his pants and grab her hand.

"Stop it!" Rebecca screamed back glaring heavily at her dad's text her and slapped away his hand.

"Stupid fucking whore!" Lorenzo muttered back, zipped up his pants and got off the couch.

Rebecca stood up, turned to Lorenzo with pure evil in her eyes; took off her heel and slapped him across the face with it. Blood oozed down Lorenzo's lips and he screamed in agonizing pain. Aaron turned down the music and the entire party shifted their attention to another one of Rebecca's ordeals. Lorenzo looked at the party goers in embarrassment and walked towards the door; he slowly creaked the door and looked down at his bloody hand from touching his busted lip. He took a few steps down the stairs and immediately turned back to the door and shouted "COPSSSSSSSSSSS!!!!" and ran back into the house.

Bruce immediately grabbed Lorenzo and gave him an uppercut causing Peter to play a game of dominos; he stumbled over a coffee table prompting him to fall on top of the couch that Peter was still passed on, which flipped over on top of a very large bag of dog food that spilled all over the ground.

"Don't fucking play that shit here, you shitty wop! Now, eat all that fucking dog food right now!" Bruce screamed in his face and pulled onto his hair.

Rebecca turned to everyone in a panic and screamed "It's true! It's true! My dad just texted me. Everyone get the fuck out!"

Lorenzo looked up at Bruce wincing in pain with a stream of tears coming down his cheeks. Bruce immediately freed him and ran to the window. Berries and cherries from the cop lights started to stalk the teenage house party. Bruce turned off all the lights and deadbolt the door, then instructed everyone they had three options: 1. Run out the backdoor towards the woods. 2. Hide in the basement and shut the hell up. 3. Run out the front door like fucking morons and get caught.

Several of the party goers elected to flee from the house including Aaron, Reggie and Travis. Bruce stayed put and continued to quiet everyone and watched five squad cars pull up to the end of the driveway. Aaron was already in the backyard ahead of his two friends and quietly screamed for them. Some of the students got arrested as Reggie and Travis ran as fast as they could; another police officer with a German Shepherd neared them by an evergreen tree.

Other students were screaming for their mommies and daddies in the distance as they got stuffed into the backseat of the squad car. A police officer ran into Bruce's house to catch anyone else hiding. Radar, the five-year-old German Shepherd, flared his jaw-sharpening teeth and barked viciously as he raced towards the three boys. The crescent moon spanked a glistening delicate reflection on Cedar Creek as barks from the angry beast ricocheted off their sneakers. The creek seemed to be the only way out; they heard others swimming for their freedom thirty feet away. Reggie screamed in fear as he quickly climbed a tree before Radar caught him. He had seen the training videos of rabid police dogs attacking men in body seats and chewing their clothing with no regard for life. Radar scratched at the bark of the tree snipping and snapping at him as he dangled from a tree branch over the beast's head.

The police were kicking over bushes and jogging through the acres of yards with their flashlights pointed calling for Radar. Travis and Aaron had located Rebecca Swanson who was in a canoe boat by the shore pleading for them to row her away from the madness. They shouted out to Reggie using his alter ego "Maxwell Hennessey"—a combination of his middle name and his mother's maiden name. They used this strategy to call out to others when they were vandalizing or were in jeopardy of being in trouble with the law to avoid parents, teachers or the police from hearing their real names.

"Guys! Let's go! What are you waiting for?" Rebecca screamed as they neared the boat. They weren't too pleased they more than likely had to cater for her needs the rest of the evening.

"Hold on, we're waiting for Maxwell," Aaron whispered as he encouraged her to keep quiet. She responded with a disgusted look on her face and started dragging the canoe to the creek herself. The creek was only fifteen feet wide and ten feet deep, but with the water temperature at fifty-nine degrees, it certainly was a little chilly for a getaway swim. Seven squad cars had shown up at the scene of the party and were starting to get closer to the perimeter of the field. Some of the younger cops had jumped into the creek and swam after a few groups pulling them back to shore.

Two police officers had reached Radar continuing to scratch at the tree and they pointed out Reggie who was now trying to climb back over to a different branch. Aaron and Travis ducked down—they saw the flashlights dart through the fields and up the tree towards Reggie. Aaron and Travis were pleading for Rebecca to put down the canoe and hide under the rocks near them to avoid getting caught, but she refused and continued to struggle to pull it towards the creek. The cops were demanding for Reggie to come down from the tree.

"Get down now! You have five seconds otherwise I'll charge you with obstruction in addition to underage drinking," one officer threatened holding up a taser in his hand. He proceeded to point it in Reggie's direction as Radar drooled sticking his tongue and gasping for air from all of the impatient barking. Aaron and Travis gulped in terror hoping for a miracle —they had escaped their funerals to lost scholarships, suspensions, and school expulsion. But to escape two nights in a row? No chance in hell. The police officer zapped a shot towards Reggie and he screamed as it nearly hit him in the face. He continued to try to find a different area in the tree to hide, but there was no hope. This was the end. Other students who were dragged from the lake continued to kick and scream in the near distance. Twenty minutes ago, they were cuffed to beer bongs. Twenty seconds ago, they were cuffed as tear songs. cons. Prisoners. Jailbirds. Convicts. Hostages.

The police officer fired another taser up the tree and it stuck Reggie. He screamed in pain, lost his balance and fell to a different branch. He hung on for his dear life as he dangled like a wounded sloth on a slippery glacier that was melting to hell. He was eventually able to crawl to the other side of the tree as he winced in discomfort and nudged a rope. Wiping the tears from his eyes, he scratched around trees and found a rope swing hidden within the tree. At last! Freedom. Could it be? He continued to untangle the rope between the branches and pulled it closer to him. The cops were now coming to the other side of the tree and one of the police officers started to climb up the tree. Reggie desperately cleared away at a few branches and could finally see the creek beneath him. He saw someone struggling to row away on the canoe and then peered down further—Aaron and Travis with their jaws dropped hiding by the rocks. Reggie tilt back and off he went touching the moonlight.

"KOWABUNGA!" Reggie squealed as he zipped on the rope swing and kicked his feet out like *George of the Jungle*. *Splash*! He went underwater and swam to the surface to hop on board with Rebecca; he eagerly grabbed one of the paddles and rowed away. Travis and Aaron immediately dove into the creek and swam after the canoe. The police officers ran toward the shore with Radar at their side barking and showing his fangs sickened that his late-night snacks had vanished away in the darkness. Aaron and Travis grabbed a paddle as well and the four of them rowed down the creek without saying a word. Radar growled and snared, crickets chirped, cops shouted, students cried and water plopped as the paddles rowed swiftly into the creek. There was a haunting silence on board the ship as the four passengers took turns paddling to freedom. They rowed for about ten miles before they felt it was safe to stop and get out.

At the neared shore Rebecca took out her phone and checked her text messages. The three boys checked their pockets but realized their phones were damaged from going into the water. The three boys shivered chattering their teeth and huddled together to try to warm up.

"Holy fuck was that water freezing! What time is it?" Travis asked Rebecca while blowing into his hands and rubbing his face.

"11:15," Rebecca replied back softy continuing to scan her messages. She looked up at them with an angry face.

"What? What's your fucking problem? We saved you," Aaron scolded ferociously rubbing his hands against his arms

"Shut up—" She snapped back.

"But...you," Aaron stuttered.

"It was the Edgewater punks. They knew Bruce was having a party and gave the cops a tip," she sighed.

"Those mother fucking pieces of shit!" Reggie bellowed and took off his shirt and drenched the water out of it.

"Such bullshit! I bet half our class got tickets tonight," Travis replied imitating Reggie's technique.

"Yeah, there is no way in they are getting away with this shit," Reggie declared.

"Well, where the fuck are we anyway?" Aaron asked as he struggled to take his polo off. Instead of unbuttoning it, he pulled it over his head but his hands got stuck in the cuffs. He cussed as he struggled in the Chinese finger trap he had just designed for himself, and flailed his hands back and forth. Finally, he got the shirt off and drenched out the soaking water.

"Edgewater," she replied looking down at the ground.

They all stared at her in disbelief as she nodded showing her blue dot on the GPS. They started to walk into the woods and heard cop sirens continuing to bleed through the crisp autumn air in the distance. Travis secretly grabbed at Rebecca's ass—she blushed back at him.

"So, can you call us a lift?" Reggie asked whipping back his shaggy hair and combing it.

"Nah, I'm not ready to go home after all of that shit. Let's steal their mascot statue. We're maybe half a mile away," Aaron interrupted.

"How would we bring it back? We gotta have a car," Travis replied.

"Ughhhh, not interested. It's time for bed. I'm calling an Uber—" Rebecca snapped back as she whipped back her hair and pulled out her phone.

"Wait. We could use your help. I don't know how heavy this thing is." Travis winked at her as he clicked out of the Uber app she had just opened up. Her face flushed a burning red while she crossed her arms frustrated that he had touched her phone. Travis breamed his bright, perfectly white smile to send a truce and her face immediately flashed a blushing pink, now delighted thinking he was hitting on her.

"Plus, we need your help. You have GPS and all of our phones are damaged. We can just throw it back to Reggie's backyard."

"Fine, but you guys owe me one." Rebecca signed as she put her phone back into her back pocket.

They decided to row the boat half a mile to their campus—easier to escape with the statue. It was a tall warrior posing in a fighting position, a crusader named Eddie Edgewater. They would have rather kidnapped the real-life mascot and beat him to a bloody pulp to send a message, but the statue would do for this evening. This time, Rebecca was keeping a watch as the three boys tugged away at the ground to remove the statue. It was a private school with lots of money, but they decided to forgo an anti-theft mechanism on it—it was on such a busy street that was heavily protected by the police and community.

They tugged at it like a dentist extracting a rotten old tooth and finally pried it out of the ground. A car was speeding by and Rebecca yelled at the boys to take cover. They held onto the statue to prevent it from tumbling over as they hid behind it. The car passed. It was a Cedar Creek police officer strolling through the neighborhood most likely looking for any other escapees from the party. The four of them struggled to carry it down and took a rest on the street.

"We gotta get the fuck out of here," Aaron said trying to heave it back up himself. They were all sweating profusely and didn't reply—they knew it was their only option. They finally got it on the canoe, laid it on its side when Eddie Edgewater in his fighting stance started to sink immediately. No more crusading, buddy!

"Fuck, fuck, fuck," Aaron screamed trying to pry it back up expecting others to help him.

"This is just as good, let him drown. I honestly have no idea where we can store that piece of shit anyway," Travis replied looking at Aaron who was trying to muscle Eddie back up to surface. Travis stood behind Rebecca as she backed her ass into his crotch. Aaron turned back over to him and she quickly shifted to her right to avoid him seeing the flirtation between the two.

"Where the fuck is Reggie?" Aaron asked, finally giving up on saving the statue and smashing his fist on the canoe.

"Probably taking a leak," Travis guessed shrugging. *THUD*! The three of them turned away and saw Reggie sliding down on his butt holding onto something.

"Ow, that fucking hurt!" he yelled and continued to lay on his back like a bug struggling to get up. He was pinned to the ground.

"Ha-ha, no you didn't!" Travis barked at him peering over at him on the ground.

"Ring, ring, the answer!" Aaron screamed helping him to his feet.

Reggie patted the sand off his jeans and stared down with the other three admiring it. Their collection for their future house parties had grown just a bit more. Aaron wiped the sand off the sign and there it was revealed.

"You got yourself a 50-point buck," Aaron declared while patting Reggie on the back and showing his awe and approval. There it laid. A big beautiful yellow Deer Crossing sign.

"Let's get this home and call it a night. I'm beat," Travis stretched and let out a yawn and high-fived Reggie for his good deed.

"What the hell do you want with that piece of junk?" Rebecca asked as she checked her phone for a new text message. "Aw damn, they canceled the homecoming dance because of Bruce's party," she groaned and typed back a reply to her phone.

"Who said that?" Reggie asked.

"My dad," she replied looking at each of them with an "ugh, oh spaghetti" expression on their faces. "He believed I was staying at Molly's place, which is a relief. But…"

"But, what?" Aaron asked. Travis turned to him with a furious frown and raised his eyebrows frustrated that he was interrupting Rebecca.

"I guess forty students got arrested and eight of them were football players. Bruce's parents are on their way back home now," she stated as the lines on her forehead slowly appeared from concern. She whipped back her hair and went silent.

"There goes our season," Aaron finally replied, continuing to stare at the sign.

"Hey, maybe it's just our bench," Reggie winced back.

"Hopefully," Travis replied staring up at the moon. "Becca, can you call us an Uber? We can fit the sign in the trunk, I'm sure."

Rebecca ordered an XL Uber to ensure they wouldn't have any trouble getting the big ol' buck into the car.

CHAPTER 8

Without phones and being grounded from the internet and television, they returned to school on Monday to learn that four of their starters were suspended for the remainder of the season. Their parents didn't refer it to grounding, they leaned more towards "witness protection" by preventing them to get into any trouble before the season ended. Being in the 21st century, even if it was for their own good, it was still a prison to not have any connection to the real world. No Facebook, Twitter, Instagram. No Netflix, Hulu, Amazon Prime or SportsCenter. Just encyclopedias, novels and their daily homework. Just law mowing, brush fires, cleaning the kitchen and helping their mothers with errands. They were promised they'd get new phones if they went to practice, stayed out of trouble in class and kept up with their schoolwork. Their parents had come a close unit themselves after the three of them became a grand trio back in middle school.

"Fuck the Faculty" week, the week after Homecoming, went on without the three of them. They set their books down from studying on school nights and heard students running through the streets celebrating with silly string and the nice warm weekend fall air. For those who weren't locked up out of the precious senior life, the vandalism of course continued. Teachers' houses were toilet papered, paint gunned, lawns douched in laundry detergent and yard furniture swapped with one neighbor to another. Aaron kept his word to Mrs. Gleason by letting her know of any tips of when she was being targeted by texting her personal number whenever he overheard someone was going to mess up her house. His D was slowly turning into a B, but as he started to fill out college applications, he felt depressed—his chances of being offered a scholarship were slowly slipping away.

Back on the football field, it was just as painful as the house arrest. It was like the entire team had gone to the dentist to fill cavities and they were infected with a near overdose of Novocain. Puffy faces, terrible sour taste in their mouths and barely able to understand each other when they spoke. They were motionless. The Pot of Gold that coach Edwards preached for weeks ago in practice was non-existent. There were no rainbows, no lucky charms nor four-leaf clovers. The coach would have been better off locking himself in a pub and drinking Guinness and Jameson until he passed out in a comatose that glued his eyelids shut forever.

Although the suspensions didn't involve their all-star players, it definitely hampered their successful start of the season. Before the party, they were a perfect 4-0. After the party, they lost their next two games and barely beat one of the weaker teams in the division by one point. They were now 5-3 and needed to most likely win their last game of the season to make the playoffs.

Travis, Reggie and Aaron were going absolutely bonkers about being locked up in their rooms all day after school. At school lunches, their faces used to light up when they heard of other students participating in debauchery activity over the weekend. But, now they could only let out a sigh and nod their heads in slow motion to appreciate the story. Before being grounded, they were the ones that boasted about how many pools and movies they snuck into, how many beer pongs they chugged and where they raced their cars over the weekend. They had to get out for just one more night before the season was over. Reggie came up with the brilliant idea to type up a fake party invitation for the seniors at the Coach's house prior to the final game. They convinced their parents it was a tradition that coach Edwards did each year to praise the work of the seniors' dedication to the team and to help jumpstart the adrenaline for the final game of the season. For many, it would be the final organized sporting event they'd be participating in for the rest of their lives.

Coach Edwards would never consider having any of his players over for dinner. In fact, it was rumored that he lived with his widowed mother and that is why he was not listed in any directory. Outside the football field, he kept to himself and often took solo trips to Lake Michigan to paint pictures of landscapes and go fishing. Reggie was great at deceiving others with his way of cheating on exams, manipulating resumes for friends and cloning templates for invitations to get himself a free pass out of doing yard work or going on weekend family getaways. On the invitation it read:

You are cordially invited to

SENIOR FAREWELL DINNER

/////////////////////^\\\\\\\\\\\\\\\\\\\\\\\

Coach Edwards is truly blessed to have had the privilege to be a part of an exciting season with the seniors of the Class of 2016. Join my family and the rest of the coaches for an honorary spaghetti on the board to show our gratitude for your hard work and dedication to the Silver Eagles football program.

TUESDAY, OCTOBER 10

7-9 PM

The Edwards Home

5525 Thunder Gulch Drive

Cedar Creek, WI

NO RSVPs. ATTENDANCE REQUIRED :)

Luckily, there were several Edwards s who resided in the community. Reggie even took the liberty to scan all of the addresses that had an Edwards residence, and chose the one that most represented where coach Edwards would live in. It was a two-story white house with green shutters and a chain fence that had a German Shepherd and Doberman consistently dashing across the front yard, greeting walkers with vicious barks as they tried to jump the fence. A confederate flag was hanging near the front window, the left side of the house had vines growing on it and the property was over an acre. The front yard was decorated with large old oak trees, gnomes and abandoned cars from the seventies. Another fence blocked the view of the backyard, but behind the house was the creek and a marsh. Although Aaron's dad didn't suspect that the invitation was a hoax, he still wanted to confirm the location of the house on Google Maps. He didn't have any doubts as the residence appeared to look like a house that coach Edwards would live in, simply based on his actions of the football field. The falsified invitation ended up working for all three—they all got a free pass from being grounded for the evening. They decided to take one extra step by looking extra spiffy and sported a nice buttoned-down shirt with khakis to flaunt in front of their parents prior to attending the dinner party.

They didn't have many hours to spare nor did they really care what they ended up doing; they simply wanted the luxury of free time they hadn't experienced in over a month. They decided to go to the Roscoe Heights Cheese Festival in one of the neighboring cities. On the drive over, they decompressed by guzzling down whiskey from flasks they were going to carry into the festival. Freedom at last. Once there, they walked around the festival and spent money on funnel cakes, cotton candy, and deep-fried Oreos. Then, they played skeeball, dart balloons and basketball.

"One more, one more!" Aaron shouted as Reggie and Travis decided it was time to head back home.

"Dude, you don't have a fucking chance. Sure, we'll watch you lose," Travis snickered and took a swig from his flask.

"Step right up, young man!" a muscular bald carnie wearing a clown costume yelled in a deep low tone from behind the counter. The man was covered in white face paint, red lipstick and black circles around his eyes. He looked started when he saw the three boys approach the counter and he reluctantly handed Aaron a miniature basketball.

"Five attempts. You gotta make three to win a prize," the carnie said in a raspy voice turning his back to them as he pointed to the game rule signs. Aaron took a few dribbles of the ball and shot his first one. Airball. The other two howled in laughter and Aaron gave them both the bird before he took his next attempt. Next one, nothing but net. Swish! Travis opened up a bag of Wildberry Skittles and poured them into his mouth as he watched on. Reggie took a quick sip from his flask and let out a violent cough.

"Pussy," Aaron muttered under his breath and made his third shot. He then missed the next attempt as it clanked around the rim.

"Rim job!" Travis snickered and poured a few more Skittles into his palm and shoved them into his mouth.

"Last shot, kid," the carnie said in the raspy voice folding his arms with his back to them.

"Book it!" Aaron yelled holding his arms up in the air after sinking his final shot.

"Whewwwwwwww. Close one," Reggie whistled and congratulated him with a high five.

"I'll take the Kamador," Aaron pointed at the moppy Hungarian sheepdog stuffed animal. The carnie quickly tossed the prize over to Aaron, took out a cigarette and walked behind his station for a smoke break.

"Jesus, what was his problem?" Travis asked as he pet Aaron's brand new prize. Aaron tossed him up in the air and caught him a few times while walking at a slow pace in a daze.

"I don't know, but why the hell did you choose that one, Aaron? You should have gotten Taz, the Tasmanian Devil. So much cooler," Reggie said sneaking another sip from his flask.

"Holy shit, guys. That carnie…" Aaron turned back to the basketball game.

"Ya?" Travis asked with his eyebrows raised.

"I think that carnie was fucking Coach Edwards," Aaron beamed.

"Ha, no way Jose, man," Reggie shouted back.

"Ya, dude. Didn't you notice he disguised his voice? He had his deep low voice right when he greeted us and then tried to avoid us as much as possible," Aaron said.

"You're out of your fucking mind. He is supposed to be serving us spaghetti on the board tonight." Travis laughed. They all turned around—he was no longer in sight. An elderly woman was now greeting the carnival goers.

"Let's get out of here," Aaron said softly picking up his pace.

"Wait, wait, not yet. Isn't that Joey "Fro Bro Show" to the right from school?" Travis asked.

"Where?" Reggie said looking near the porta-potty area.

"9 o'clock. Jesus, don't look all at once. Looks like he is with his parents. Ha, let's get that fucker and then scram."

"Man, we don't have enough time," Aaron replied throwing up his prized stuffed animal again. "I want to drop this over at my niece's tonight."

"Does your niece have you by the balls?" Travis snapped back.

"No, shithead, but it'll help with my parents maybe giving me a break," Aaron replied.

"Just do it tomorrow, it doesn't have to be done tonight. Plus, why the hell would you go to your aunt's house after a team dinner? It would just be plain fuckery for all of us," Travis said as he tiptoed around one of the carnival games so he wouldn't be seen by Joey. He was a short, scrawny white nerdy kid with glasses complemented with freckles, acne, dandruff, rosacea, and terrible body odor. No compliments coming his way anytime soon. His father was a police officer for the community, but that didn't stop him from being bullied by everyone in the school.

"I'm just going to use the jon quick and then I'll meet you over to buy the snacks," Joey called out to his parents.

"Okay, hurry up, Joey." His dad called back holding his wife's hand while walking away.

"What are you going to do?" Reggie snickered.

"Going to need another one of you, fellas," Travis laughed and took one more sip of liquid courage.

"I'm in. Plus he's gotta protect his precious niece's toy anyway," Reggie snickered and pointed at Aaron who rolled his eyes back. Travis whispered something into Reggie's ear who rolled with laughter. "Get a head start and run to the car, Aaron.

This one is going to get real messy." Reggie rubbed his hands together in excitement.

"Ready, set, break," Travis declared as they ran over near Joey. They quickly bought some masks from a carnie to disguise their face and snuck behind a merry-go-round as they watched Joey look at his watch while waiting to go to the bathroom. A man walked out of the porta-potty he was waiting for and he held the door for Joey who walked in. He covered the toilet with sheets and sat down. Moments later, Travis and Reggie ran over to the porta-potty and drop kicked it as hard as they could. It swayed to the right and rocked back and forth while Joey held out his hands on both sides of the porta-potty to try to stay up. Reggie and Travis quickly got back to their feet and both performed a spear on the porta-potty dropping it over on its side. They let out a hideous laugh and ran towards the cornfields, back towards the car. Poor Joey tried to go to a neighboring town with the purpose to enjoy himself with his family, but the location didn't matter. Wherever he went, he was always tormented.

"Ahhhhhhhhhhhhhhhhhhhhhhhhhhh what the fuck!" Joey screamed in horror covered in shit from head to toe. He tried to plug his nose while other carnival goers ran to his rescue and pulled him out. Aaron was overlooking from afar and his jaw dropped as he witnessed the cruel prank that his best friends pulled on the one and only "Fro Bro Show." He watched them dart across the fields of corn as others chased after them.

"Get the fuck back here punks! That was absolutely uncalled for!" a woman carnie yelled at the boys shaking her fist in the air. Joey was unlocked from his coffin of feces and he let out a whale that could have been heard from miles away. His hair, glasses, shirt, socks and entire skin were covered in shit. A few people were laughing, shedding him even more embarrassment. His dad ran over with a towel to wipe him down and comfort his son. He handed him a soda and Joey angrily swiped it away into the air.

"I hope those fucking assholes rot in hell," Joey's father said looking over at the cornfields with his wife now behind him tearing up herself.

Aaron decided to run back to the car as fast as he could. Seconds later, he overheard a generator switch go off and the entire festival went pitch black. Moans and screams were heard across the park. People were running in every direction scared for their lives. Aaron could no longer see where he was going and feared he would get caught—he wouldn't be able to find his way back to the car. He didn't have access to his cellphone since he was still being grounded from it.

"Let's grab this quick while we can," Reggie whispered.

"Fuck yes, easy target," Travis replied.

"Avery, where the fuck are you?" Reggie silently called out Aaron's middle name to the cornfields. Fearing that he'd been heard, he didn't respond and started to run in the direction towards where he could hear Reggie and Travis continuing to cause mischief. *PLOP!* A loud thud of something hitting the ground as a car door opened. Aaron finally reached the road and a car quickly flashed its headlights on him. He ran over to the car and jumped into the backseat with his stuffed animal.

"Go, go, go!" Aaron screamed. Travis noticed there were now several people crossing the street, so he put the car in reverse and went backyards over fifty miles per hour towards a back road to flee the scene.

"Now, that's what I call a fucking spaghetti dinner with meatballs," Travis howled in laugher as Reggie smashed his fists on the dashboard in excitement. Aaron turned to his right and noticed there was a fifth passenger in the car [a Do Not Enter sign sitting next to his Kamador} with him and could only let out a sigh.

"How do you and the pup like the company back there?" Reggie turned around letting out a laugh. "We're calling that one, Joey!" Reggie turned back around and Aaron showed a frown that he needed to camouflage in the dark from his friends. He felt a little ashamed of what his friends had done to the poor kid. He certainly didn't deserve to be Humpty Dumpty while humping over to do his business in the dump.

CHAPTER 9

Senior Night for the Silver Eagles came in mid-October. The shades of brown, yellow, orange, red leaves covered the autumn horizon, families were out preparing for Halloween buying the customs, decorations, pumpkins, fake cobwebs the bulk of candy while the aroma of sweet cinnamon apple pie and pumpkin spice lattes filled classrooms and office rooms around the Cedar Creek community. The evening was filled with clashing thunderstorms, strong winds and bolts of lightning. A final blast of humidity arrived as summer was kicking and screaming to survive one final day within the fall season.

"We got this shit! We got this shit!" Bruce screamed as he pet the rabbit leg for good luck in his locker. BOOM! Loud lightning blasted near the football field and the lights flickered.

"They are keeping us in here for another twenty minutes or so until it's safe out there," Coach Edwards announced as he walked over to the team trying to get amped up. "For fucking sake, let's win this God damn game tonight so we can make the playoffs. If we make the tournament, we'll finally have the entire unit back cleared from suspensions. THERE WILL BE NO LET DOWNS!" he screamed and spit came flying out of his mouth. "You know damn well that I'm still pissed at all of you for nearly sacrificing your own futures, your scholarship opportunities and more importantly…. my respect," he bellowed and sat down on the bench to stare at them in the face waiting for a response.

"Maybe we will never be forgiven for our actions last month, but we will also never be forgotten for our actions this evening. We will crawl on broken glass to the goal-line if we have to. We won't give up. We won't surrender. That is our home out there. That is our life out there. We owe this to Coach. We owe this for ourselves. Let's fucking rock and roll and flock and soul. Hillcrest will eat our bird shit tonight if they like it or not," Aaron preached as he grabbed his rabbit foot out of his locker and put it in the air. Everyone else joined in and raised their fists with their rabbit feet and screamed "LET'S GO EAGLES!" several times at the top of their lungs. No one on the team noticed from being so amped up, but Coach Edwards had shed a tear as he sat down on the bench and clapped his hands supporting Aaron's speech.

The thunder and the lightning finally passed and the team ran out of the locker room like the energizer bunny amped up on five liters of Mountain Dew. Every possible emotion ran through their bodies as they high-fived classmates, parents, faculty running onto the field smashing through their banner. Coach Edwards jogged behind the team shouting out support with a frog in his throat. He had done so much screaming and throwing foreign objects in the locker room that he had nearly lost his voice a few times.

The game remained tight throughout the first three quarters and the Hillcrest Tigers held a 21-15 lead going into the last seven minutes of the football game. The Silver Eagles were struggling to get into the end zone and had converted on five of their six field goal attempts. On the last attempt, their kicker's leg was broken after he was tackled hard by a linebacker when they tried to do a fake field goal to tie up the game. Instead of being down by a field goal, they were now down by a touchdown. The turf was also severely soaked so it made it difficult for Travis to get traction and escape the pocket when he was being targeted by the defensive line.

The Tigers had possession of the ball and were starting to march down the field with now only four minutes left in the game; the Silver Eagles only had one timeout left. They had converted on three consecutive third downs like it was a cakewalk. The quarterback for the Tigers was starting to taunt the defensive line as he took his precious time to break from huddles to kill more time off the clock. The Silver Eagles desperately needed to make a defensive stop otherwise their hopes for playoff contention, a state championship, and maybe even scholarships, would all wash away in the storm.

"Time out! Time out! Atwood!" Coach Edwards yelled as he violently chewed on some gum and blew a bubble. Aaron ran over to him with his helmet.

"Yes, Coach?"

"I'm going to put you as one of the corners. We have to stop this aerial attack immediately," he screamed as the Tigers converted on yet another first down. Aaron immediately ran onto the field and yelled to the other cornerback calling for a substitution. Travis and Reggie had their heads down, looked up in shock and ran closer to the sideline to get a glimpse of what they were seeing. Aaron had never played a defensive position in his life.

"Down…. Set…. Oh wait! Look at Mr. Big Shot trying to save the day," the opposing tight end called out pointing at Aaron on the ride sideline. No time to queue the Jeopardy music. Time was of the essence. Aaron looked over glaring at him agitated, paranoid and electrified all at once.

"Gold Dust! Gold Dust!" the quarterback called for an audible and one of the receivers ran in motion towards the side of the field Aaron was guarding. The receiver was their biggest threat and he stood at 6' 4"--rather tall for a high-school wideout. One minute and twelve seconds remained on the clock. They were on the forty-five-yard line, just one more first down from being in field goal territory. It was third down and three yards to go. This was for all the marbles. If they didn't stop this third down, every last marble would instead be caught in their throats for the rest of their lives. Suffocation. Misery. Defeat.

The quarterback snapped the ball and the receiver ran a "Stop and Go" route. Aaron jumped on the pump fake to the wideout that he was now covering. The quarterback threw a perfect spiral and connected on the fifteen-yard line and the Tigers receiver bolted towards the end zone. Aaron looked in terror and imagined Radar, the German Shepherd, running at him chomping at his sneakers. The students and fans on Tigers bleachers were jumping up and down and the band was beginning to chant their victory song. Coach Edwards threw his clipboard down and fell backward on his ass covering his eyes in horror. The rest of the team dropped to their knees as their unsaved hopes and dreams flooded their young, innocent faces sobbing with no remorse. The kind where you weep so much it begins to sting like you are doused in honey trapped in a beehive with one thousand queens.

POP! The football flew out of the receiver's hands just before he touched the goal line. Aaron had caught up to him at the last second and caused a fumble. The receiver turned around shocked looking for the ball when Aaron hurdled on top of it in the middle of the end zone. He hugged it like he hadn't seen it in decades and started to tear up. They weren't playing inside a dome. But if they would have been, the roof would have been blown off and landed on Mars. The Silver Eagle fans had erupted and everyone was running back and forth screaming their faces off high-fiving everyone. Those that had snuck alcohol into the stadium swigged and swigged and swigged on their flasks. Others were watching the prep football game at a local pub a few blocks away and were slamming on the bar table with everyone taking shots.

But it wasn't over. It was far from over. It was only a save from humiliating defeat on their own home field on Senior Night. Aaron slowly crawled to his feet clutching the football to his side and ran back towards the sideline to greet the pandemonium. Aaron's ears started to ring as he neared—he was immediately shoved in excitement; he tried to keep his balance like a bowling pin on its last wind.

"You're my fucking hero!" Coach Edwards screamed and a bucket of spit came flying from his mouth. His piece of gum dropped to the ground; he picked it up and flung it up the air and morphed into a child smiling like he just found a puppy under his tree during Christmas morning. It was now time to take the field with fifty-eight seconds remaining and no time-outs.

For the first play, they ran a hook and ladder, and Travis converted for twenty-five yards after Reggie pitched the ball back for him. They were now on their own forty-five-yard line with forty-one seconds left. Travis screamed for everyone to get to the back of the line so he could spike the ball. Travis yelled for the ball, but Bruce, the center, put too much mustard on the toss and it flew through Travis's hands. FUMBLE! Aaron ran from the other side of the field and blocked three people preventing them from falling on top of the ball. Reggie jumped on the ball as the rest of the team screamed to get back to the line to call a play.

It was now third down and thirty-seven yards to go with twenty-eight seconds on the clock and running. Travis threw a quick out route to Aaron who caught it and immediately stepped out of bounds to stop the clock with twenty-one seconds left. It was now fourth down and this was more than likely the final play of the game. The team had to go seventy-two more yards in the next fourteen seconds. Travis called a play and it looked like he was running a hail Mary. They instead ran a Statue of Liberty play and Reggie took the ball from Travis's hands and ran as fast as he could near the sideline as he zoned into the game clock. With four seconds left, he leaped out of bounds and the team was now at the twenty-three-yard line. It was a genius play call by Coach Edwards to allow for additional yardage, that way Travis didn't have to heave the ball from over fifty yards away to the end zone.

The Hillcrest Tigers called timeout to strategize how they would defend the final play of the game and to prevent the Cedar Creek Silver Eagles from making the playoffs. Coach Edwards quickly got everyone in a quick huddle and called for Aaron to play the quarterback position. Travis looked over at Aaron and gave his nod of approval and then strapped on his helmet to take the field as a wideout.

"Down, set, hut!" Aaron shouted as Bruce hiked the ball. Aaron stepped deep back in the pocket as the Tigers unleashed an unexpected full out blitz. Aaron ran in circles, ducking, zig-zagging, pump faking and stiff arming his way from being feasted on by the Tigers. The offensive linemen tried to continue to protect the prey, but wanted to avoid being called for a holding penalty. "Run, you fuckers!" Aaron yelled as he used his line as protection shoving them into defenders. He realized he didn't have an opportunity to throw the ball into the end zone and his best option was to attempt to run in the end zone.

Aaron reached the eight-yard line and was just about to be tackled from behind by two Tigers. Reggie and Travis came to his rescue at the last second and viciously blocked them right on their asses. Aaron now just had the safety who was waiting for him near the end zone. Aaron hurdled over the safety, but was met by other defenders that caught up. As Aaron dove into the air, he stuck out the football as far as he could to cross the plane for a touchdown. The referees looked at each other trying to determine if he made it in the end zone or not—they cleared the rest of the football players from the area. The entire stadium was silent; they had no idea which emotion they were supposed to be feeling at that very moment.

All referees joined in unison glancing over the football as Aaron stayed flat on the ground holding onto the end of the football right at the goal line. The head referee quickly conversed with his colleagues and walked forward as he halted the most beautiful signal that could ever be seen on a Friday evening. TOUCHDOWN! Aaron started to tear up as the rest of his teammates ran over and did baseball slides in his direction to avoid piling on him like they had done in a previous game.

The band began to blast magnificent victory tunes, the students bellowed student chants, the Hillcrest Tigers walked off their field with their tails between their legs, college recruiters stood up applauding and Aaron's dad threw popcorn in his mouth as he screamed at the top of his lungs "God dammit, that's my fucking son! Go Aaron!" Aaron's mom looked over at him in dismay, crossing her arms while shaking her head but let out a grin and gave him a big smooch right smack dab on his lips.

CHAPTER 10

That evening, Aaron's parents decided to rejoice by having Reggie and Travis's family over for homemade pizza and a bonfire. The Silver Eagles had found the pot of gold Coach Edwards referred to at the start of the season. Playoffs? Yes, we're talking about playoffs.

As the mothers were in the kitchen making the pizzas, the rest of the gang sat around watching the news and waiting for the highlights of one of the most magical moments of their lives. Aaron's older brother, Tyler, was also home for the next few days on a business trip. The home was nice and cozy with the fireplace roasting: Teddy was chewing on a rawhide in the middle of the floor, pictures of a blossoming family were all throughout the house and the aroma of apple cinnamon candles burning as the stars glittered outside the window still made the night even more magical. The last few weeks had been very miserable for the boys. The winter blues had come three months earlier, but now it seemed like everything was falling back into a place. The three boys were back together nestled in Aaron's living room, spending quality time with the family and fully enjoying the playoff berth.

"I think I'm okay with having these fellas have a celebratory cigar after dinner," Reggie's dad said swigging a beer and gave Reggie a noogie. Reggie laughed, scooted away and took a sip of his Dr. Pepper.

"Oh, most definitely. These boys deserve it." Aaron's dad, Austin agreed as he sat back comfortably in his reclining chair with his hands behind his head and a gigantic smile on his face.

"I actually had that on my mind before we came over here. Went down to my humidor and got six Arturo Fuentes," Travis's dad announced, leaned over and flashed the box of cigars with a grin. He had accidentally spilled beer on his shirt due to all the excitement, and everyone let out a laugh.

"Ha-ha. Dad, you're such a klutz," Travis said clapping his hands with joy and taking a glance at the box of cigars.

"I'm going to definitely have to come back down for the playoffs. That game tonight was better than NFL Sunday Ticket, boys," Tyler hoisted his glass of whiskey, clinked it to the father's and took a swig.

"Honey! Honey! Get over here! They are about to show the highlights." Austin yelled leaning over to face the kitchen as he hushed the rest of the men in the living room. A one-minute clip of all the spectacular plays lit up the 70-inch flat-screen

TV mounted on their wall. The three boys shook each other in delight humming the tune of the "SportsCenter." After the sports section was over, everyone high-fived each other and the mothers went back to the kitchen.

"Let's see what good movies are on tonight," Austin said taking a swig of beer and grabbing the remote to change the channel.

"We continue to receive reports that street signs have been stolen from multiple areas in Cedar Creek. No suspects have been identified and the police are urging residents to call in if you have any information that leads to an arrest," a blonde anchor reported. Aaron's dad held the remote to his stomach raising his eyebrows confused. The mothers stood near the entrance of the kitchen to also tune into the segment.

"This has been an issue in the past and we're fully invested in exploring additional resources to stop this crime from happening in our community. These signs are here to protect our residents and it is a felony to steal signs that hinder the safety of Cedar Creek. We strongly encourage anyone that has been involved or knows anyone that has been involved to step forward so we can ensure all residents and anyone passing through Cedar Creek is fully protected with the street signage present throughout our community," Officer Adams scuffed.

He stared into the camera with his thick mustache and sunglasses clipped to his uniform. It was the same officer that unleashed Radar and attempted to shoot Reggie with a taser the night they escaped on the canoe from Bruce's party.

The three boys glanced at each other in disbelief their recklessness had made the news. They had made the news twice in one evening. Once for finding the pot of gold and making the playoffs, and another for being thieves and becoming the communities snot and mold. Their parents didn't know they still had snuck out on a couple of occasions to steal signs. Travis had mapped out a list of all the signs he wanted to collect so they could be used as decorations for their upcoming college parties. So far they had retrieved the following: Dead End, Deer Crossing, 55 MPH, Railroad Crossing, Yield, Do Not Enter, No Parking, Road Work Ahead and Reserved Parking. They decided the only other ones they needed to add were a Stop Sign and the street signs for the roads of their last names which all existed within their town: Atwood (Aaron), Burner (Reggie) and Connery (Travis). When they were younger, they would dance around in the basement of each other homes to Jackson 5 "ABC" because their last names together had the beginning of the alphabet.

"The community is also asking for donations to help insert RFD devices into our signage to prevent theft from continuing to happen," the blonde anchor said.

"That's some odd shit. Who the hell would want a bunch of street signs?" Travis' dad yelled throwing his hands up in the air.

"I'll be damned," Travis' mother said, shaking her head at the TV.

"You boys don't know anyone that has been stealing those signs, do you?" Reggie's mom asked. She took a sip of her red wine and threw back her hair.

"Nuh, uh. Like, how could you even store them somewhere. They are pretty huge I thought," Travis lied with an honest face and took a sip of Dr. Pepper.

"Welp. Let's go eat." Austin clapped his hands and turned off the TV. They all walked into the kitchen taking their seats and preparing to feast on a scrumptious meal. Light relaxing music played in the background and the Halloween decorations and signs that were hanging danced around the kitchen. Aaron scratched Teddy's ears and let out a grin looking at the "This kitchen is seasoned with Love" sign that was perfectly placed above the oven. It was a gift he had given to his mother last

Christmas and he was very pleased that she was so happy with it.

"Bon Appetit," Donna said smiling and passing around the dishes of Napoleon pizza, Mediterranean salad and breadsticks.

"What are you boys up to this evening?" Travis' dad said biting into a piece of pizza.

"I guess we'll stay here and babysit you!" Travis laughed and pointed at the pizza sauce that covered his father's face.

"Oh, my goodness, we forgot your bib," Travis' mother snickered taking a drink of red wine and the entire kitchen laughed.

"We'll probably watch a movie here tonight if that's okay?" Aaron asked going in for a second slice of pizza.

"Jesus, Chestnut. Slow down, buddy." Tyler laughed referring to Joey Chestnut, a competitive world eater who was notoriously known for scarfing down seventy-plus hot dogs in Coney Island during the Fourth of July weekend. Aaron smiled back, dipped his slice of pizza into some ranch and took a big bite.

"Yes, that's fine by me," Donna replied. "Teddy, get down!" she then yelled as the goofy mongrel tried inviting himself as a guest to the pizza. The table roared with laughter, Aaron pulled him away and threw a treat to the living room to keep him away from the food.

"When the moon hits your eye like a big pizza pie," they all sang together when Dean Martin came on Aaron's playlist. More laughter. More harmony. More freedom. No more solitary. Life was good, great, grand and no one could take it away from them. That evening the boys knew they wouldn't be watching any movies. STOP SIGN bled deep in their brains. No plans were needed. It was destiny.

The boys volunteered to clean the kitchen and everyone gave "oohs and awes" impressed with the help. But, of course it was only offered so they could discuss their game plan for the steal later that evening.

"Which one should we target?" Travis asked and let Teddy lick some pizza sauce off one of the plates.

"How about the one at the Dunwoody and Damascus intersection?" Travis asked.

"Yeah, that's perfect. I mean, Dunwoody runs right into that huge embankment so if you don't stop there regardless of a sign being there, you'd have to be a complete dumbass. I don't see this being a big deal at all," Aaron replied pouring in the soap for the dishwasher.

"Yeah, plus it's not that busy of an intersection. It's oncoming traffic going fifty-five MPH on Damascus, so everyone knows they have to wait for cars before turning left or right. This is going to be great!" Reggie laughed to Teddy resting his two front paws on the door of the dishwasher to try to get a couple more licks of the plates before it was closed.

"Don't let him do that," Aaron's dad said walking past the kitchen holding a cigar in his mouth motioning for them to come outside.

"Teddy, get down boy." Aaron pulled him off by his collar and closed the dishwasher shut and started it.

They went outside and joined their fathers for cigars. In the future, they'd celebrate their first homes, marriages and the birth of their first child. But tonight it was celebrating the final chapters of their own childhood. As they blew smoke from their mouths and coughed violently from the strong expensive cigars, their fathers and Tyler chuckled and took swigs from their beers. They were capturing what they'd potentially be like twenty years from that moment. Aaron's dad was a high-school teacher, Reggie's dad was a general manager of several grocery stores around the area, and Travis's dad was a welder. Tyler was the big shot lawyer and helped them with providing financial advice for investments, which always seemed to be accurate recommendations as they all were fairly successful and were able to support their families with no problem.

"So, what movie are you watching tonight, fellas?" Tyler asked as he puffed on his cigar sitting on the stairs dumping his ashes into a beer car.

"Not sure yet. Probably a comedy," Travis replied.

"Oh yeah? I could go for a good comedy. Be right back, gotta take a leak" Tyler said patting Aaron on the shoulder, took a swig of beer and left to go the bathroom. Aaron, sighed causing his hair to briefly stick up, rolled his eyes at Reggie and Travis knowing that the additional guest to their non-existent movie party was going to put a damper on their plans.

The other two families departed and Aaron's parents headed off to bed. The three boys and Tyler went into the living room and sprawled out on the couches as Aaron scrolled through Netflix to find a good movie that they'd all enjoy. Aaron decided on *Step Brothers* starring Will Ferrell and John C. Reilly. It was a movie they had seen several times, but it was a classic feel-good movie that no one could ever resist. Tyler returned to the living room with four bowls of popcorn and handed them out to everyone.

"Thanks, Tyler!" Travis replied grabbing the bowl from him and stuffing popcorn in his mouth. Pieces of popcorn fell onto the couch. He leaned over to his right searching for the hidden popcorn and ate them one by one by pulling them from the crevices of the couch.

"Like father, like son. Be right back." Tyler laughed and walked out of the living room. He was still wearing his business attire and his hair was parted to the right. He was a tall, slender man with nice well-kept nails that his wife manicured every week. Well-dressed, clean groomed and smelling good was something that the Atwood's always thrived for.

The boys shoved popcorn into their mouths and howled with laughter as Will Ferrel and John C. Reiley argued in the movie *Step Brothers.*

"Look, I didn't touch your drum set, okay?"

"I witnessed with my eyes your testicles touching my drum set."

Tyler returned to the room with tall four large frozen glasses and set them on the coffee table where Teddy was lying underneath. Teddy was wagging his tail and slowly drifted into sleep. Reggie pointed at the glasses wondering what they were being used for.

"Root beer floats. The perfect complement to the seasoned popcorn you guys got there." Tyler laughed and slapped his knees with a huge smile.

"Ahh, okay. Where is it?" Travis asked confused.

"You know what's crazy? It's already been five years since my high-school team was state runner-ups." Tyler pointed at a picture on the wall of him as a teenage boy hoisting the second-place trophy. "Man, we were so fucking close, it still bugs the shit out of me to this day. If it wasn't for this bullshit, it was a guarantee we would have won State." Tyler then pointed to the previously ruptured ACL that may have prevented him from becoming a professional football player.

"Yeah man, it would have been so sweet to see you slinging touchdowns in the NFL," Reggie said while eating more popcorn.

"Thanks, Reg. But, now it's your guys' time to shine." Tyler straightened his posture and reached behind him. The three of them tried to peek behind to see what he was grabbing. Four dark delicious bottles of German Dunkel. Tyler popped off the caps and passed them to the three boys who desperately held their hands out like they were begging for candy on Halloween.

"Trick-or-treat," Aaron snickered; Travis poured the scrumptious beer into his glass and tilted it back to ensure it wasn't filled with a foam head.

"Don't tell your mothers about me giving you guys these beers. But, I felt you needed a celebratory beer, not just a cigar." Tyler lifted his glass of beer and they all clinked and shouted "Prost" and took a big swig. Tyler hushed them and let out laughter. Aaron pressed play, they sat back and watched the movie while they waited for Tyler to drift away. Halfway through the movie, the three boys leaned their heads and peaked over to Aaron's older brother. Tyler was passed out cold, snoring with his feet up on the coffee table and his glass of beer half empty. Aaron grabbed it, took a swig and he passed it around until it was gone. Teddy awoke and let out a yawn, stretched and let himself out the doggy door in the fenced-in backyard.

"Let's scram! Wham! Bam! Thank you, Ma'am!" Aaron whispered in silence carefully picking up his keys from the coffee table that were lying adjacent to his brother's feet.

They walked out to the garage. Reggie pulled a chainsaw from the rack and hopped into Aaron's Cutlass Supreme. Travis followed behind carrying a twelve-pack of beer and a bottle of whiskey they had hidden by the side of the fridge. It wasn't alcohol they had bought themselves nor was it stolen from their parents. Instead, it was stolen from fridges around the community while they were deployed in a game called "Brandon Mission."

If they were running low on funds, the three of them would tag team together to steal beers from neighbors. It was a secret genius strategy they developed while locked up in solitary at their own homes during the early part of the football season. They vouched to never tell anyone else of this secret, even their own teammates. If it leaked, somehow someway it would be pinned back on them.

The scoop on Brandon Missions? The three of them would drive in the Cutlass Supreme patrolling neighborhoods where they wouldn't be noticed and look for homes that had their garage door open. Aaron would park the car five to ten homes down the street and be on the lookout for anyone pulling up the driveway of the house they were targeting. Travis and Reggie would steadily walk up to a house in broad daylight. Reggie would ring the doorbell and Travis would hide on the side of the garage peering over at Reggie. Once, someone answered the door; Reggie would introduce himself as Maxwell and say he was looking for someone named Brandon who lived at the residence. Several people would immediately say, "Sorry, but you have the wrong house," but Reggie would swiftly insist that it was the address he was given and pull out a piece of paper with Brandon's name and the address they were both standing at. Meanwhile, Travis would sneak into the garage and steal any alcohol the homeowners had in their possession (if they had a fridge in the garage). Cold delicious beer, wine coolers, bottles of liquor, you name it. After Reggie finally apologized that he realized he was at the wrong house, he'd meet up with Travis down the street where Aaron would quickly pick them up and drive off down the street as they cracked a beer to celebrate the success of the "Brandon Mission."

One time it got a little scary, though. Reggie was fibbing to a neighbor he knew a Brandon who had lived in the house in the past and was telling childhood stories to keep the elderly woman at the door. Meanwhile, her husband had shut the garage door and Travis had to hide under one of the cars so that he wouldn't be seen. Travis had been stuck inside for thirty minutes and the elderly woman was no longer amused with Reggie and threatened to call the police if he didn't get off their property. Travis texted pleading to Aaron and Reggie to come out with a solution—he had to meet with Angela for their third anniversary dinner. Reggie and Travis jokingly texted back that the garage was where he made the reservations for the dinner. They then sent a picture of themselves smiling laughed and slurped down cold refreshing beer. Travis lost it and came out with a game plan himself. He looked up the phone number in the yellow pages on his phone of the residence they were at, blocked his cellphone number and called the house.

"Hello?" the elderly woman said softly on the phone.

"Your grandson has been murdered," Travis said in a deep raspy voice. Click.

"Sherman!" The woman cried at the top of her lungs to her husband. Travis heard another person run up to the staircase, crawled from underneath the car and ran through their kitchen bolting out the backdoor and jumped into the car. He immediately grabbed one of the cans of beer sitting in the backseat of the Cutlass and explained the escape route with a menacing smile. Aaron and Reggie disgustingly gulped their throats; their pupils dilated, hands tremored and sweated profusely from their foreheads frozen in silence. They tried to avoid talking about it—it was such a harsh thing to do. Coincidently, a boy named Toby in their class never showed up at school again after that day.

CHAPTER 11

Reggie cradled the chainsaw in the backseat like a baby, Travis passed out the beers and Aaron timed out the ten-minute drive on his GPS to Dunwoody and Damascus. This evening was going to solidify their sweet stolen street sign scheme. They agreed this would be their last collective effort, but they had to seal the deal individually by snatching the street signs with their last names on a recon mission. Aaron slammed his hands on the dashboard, guzzled down beer, and blasted *Highway to Hell* by ACDC

"Woooooooooooo!" Aaron screamed with his head out the window. "Let's take a quick detour!" He tapped in the Edgewater quarterback's address into the GPS. Travis clapped his hands together in delight and shouting "Highway to hell!" while Reggie pretended to play guitar on his chainsaw in the backseat. They all head-banged to the music and chucked their empty beer cans out the window. They were indeed on the highway to hell. Not for themselves, but for every single person in their path. No roadblocks (they had "Dead End" Reggie with them). No speed limits. No stoplights.

They pulled up to Adam Drexel's s house and Aaron pointed back at Reggie nodding to do the dirty deed. Reggie started up the chainsaw and the mailbox went flying into the bushes. The lights came on in the house and someone ran down the street with their shirt off. They were already gone. The smell of the rubber on the tire burst Adam's nostrils as he picked up the red postal flag that was laying on the ground, chucked it and screamed "God Damnit!" Several football players lived on the same block so they decided Reggie would be the lumberjack of the neighborhood and clear the entire forest one mailbox by one.

"I think we just got enough gas left for the stop sign," Reggie heckled in the backseat throwing another finished beer can out the window.

They approached the intersection and Aaron flicked his high beam lights off and on the sign. Aaron pulled the car over behind some trees so it couldn't be seen by passing cars. They all got out of the car and stood there in silence looking like they were *Jack* and the stop sign was an enormous bean stalk reaching into the clouds. This was the last steal. What would they do for shenanigans after this adventure was complete? They convinced themselves they'd focus on their schoolwork, but they knew they'd crash and burn with a spell of suffocating, sadistic senioritis just like every other schoolmate later in the year.

Aaron got the honor this time: his glorious defensive stop and game-winning touchdown earlier in the evening. He revved up the chainsaw and the stop sign fell to the ground within seconds. Such a much wiser decision to transition from using a handsaw to a chainsaw over the past few months. They all stared at the ground and huddled over the stop sign as if it was a beached whale with no hope to survive.

"Down, set, hut!" Travis screamed, stepped back, gave a fake handoff to Reggie and threw him a beer. Reggie grabbed another beer from his pocket and crushed both beers together like former WWE wrestler, "Stone Cold" Steve Austin; the delicious golden liquid violently oozed all over his face and mouth. He threw the beer cans into the field, then the three of them picked up the stop sign and put it in the backseat. They all hopped into the Cutlass. Aaron started the engine and pulled out from beneath the trees. They started to drive down the back road and turned around to hear a truck speeding down the street towards them. Travis and Reggie cried for Aaron to put the foot on the pedal—they knew it was someone from the Edgewater football team hunting them down.

The truck started to tailgate them—the driver was blaring his horns and flashing his high beams. There was another person in the passenger side wailing his hands, waving for them to pull over. Every time the truck tried to get on the side of the Cutlass, Aaron would step on the pedal and shift back and forth to the right to prevent the truck from passing him.

"Just let him pass, dude!" Travis screamed.

"They don't want to pass us! They want to kill us for fucking up their mailboxes," Aaron clutched the steering wheel and bit down hard on his lip until it bled. It had become foggy and it was getting more difficult to see the road ahead.

"Just pull over!" Reggie yelled from the backseat. "We have a chainsaw if they try anything on us."

"Don't be fucking stupid!" Aaron wiped the windshield with his sleeve to try to get more visibility. Now, the truck was violently blaring on the horn and nudging on Aaron's tail. Aaron looked back, rolled down his window and gave the truck the bird.

"Dude, slow down!" Travis shrieked as he grabbed the wheel. They were approaching a huge curve in the road and Aaron took his foot off the gas. Within seconds, a deer jumped out in the middle of the street. Aaron hit it and came to a rapid halt. The truck slammed on its brakes behind them and both of the passengers immediately ran out of their cars up to Aaron's window. They pounded on the window as the three boys looked out their windshield—the deer lay motionless in the middle of the road. Dead as meat.

Reggie started to rev up the chainsaw and got out of the backseat. Aaron and Travis pleaded for him to stay inside the car, but he wouldn't have it. He unlocked the backseat after they tried to keep the door locked several times.

"Bruce!? Nelson!" he squealed as he opened the door with the chainsaw. He then ran violently towards their chests. They put their hands up and backed away slowly. Reggie realized he looked like a psychopath on a murdering spree—he quickly turned off the chainsaw and set it down on the ground.

"What the fuck are you guys doing out here?" Bruce asked as Travis and Reggie got out of the car and turned off the engine.

"We were getting some revenge on the Edgewater fucks. We thought you were them because we fucked with their mailboxes." Travis drank from a can of beer. They all paused and realized the deer was dead and Aaron had damaged the hood of his car. They walked over to the side of the car and noticed there was another gigantic crack in the windshield; Chronic wasting disease (CDC) was oozing off the car into a pool of Rudolph blood. Bruce peered into the backseat.

"How the fuck didn't you guys recognize Bruce's truck? I mean come on! Everyone knows this baby! We thought you guys were Edgewater shitheads too so we were chasing you. They just egged the shit out of our houses. Probably seventy miscarried chickens splattered all over our houses. My parents were so pissed they called the cops and they are talking to them now," Nelson said leaning against Bruce's Chevy Silverado. Although Bruce gave Nelson and his younger brother Peter a lot of shit, they were still very close friends; their mothers worked together at the hospital for several years.

"Jesus fucking Christ!" Bruce screamed pointing at the stop sign that was barely covered by the alcohol in the backseat. "You guys will be in deep shit if you keep that. What do you want with it anyway?"

Aaron shared their story of the street sign decoration they were going to have at their house parties and both Bruce and Nelson agreed it was an awesome idea. They requested to be invited to their first party. Travis and Reggie dragged the dead carcass and threw it off the side of the road.

"We got to get the hell out of here." Travis cried and wiped blood onto his t-shirt. "We look like we were just involved in a massive blood bath."

"Only you," Bruce jabbed back looking at everyone's shirts.

"I'm fucking serious. Let's go!" Travis yelled.

"Wait, wait!" Bruce massaged his thick, scruffy beard and took another look at the stop sign. "Did you guys check to see if there are stickers on that thing?"

"Stickers?" Aaron looked at the stop sign.

"Yeah, didn't you guys hear they are trying to stop the theft of all these signs? How many people are doing this with you guys?" Bruce opened the door to examine the stop sign.

"Yeah, we heard. Figured it was just a bluff to scare people off. As far as I know, it's just us doing it," Reggie said.

"Guys, we can't be out here in the middle of the road like this," Travis begged and got into the passenger seat signaling Reggie and Aaron to do the same.

"Oh, fuck me sideways and call me Marry Poppins," Bruce shrieked and rubbed his finger over the sticker. "This son of a bitch has been tagged. I saw some land surveyors out here earlier so must've been today."

"Well, can't we just remove it?" Aaron questioned Bruce.

"Nope, don't think so." Bruce spit out a big wad of chew on the ground. "Shit, there is a cop near here. Chuck that fucking thing and follow me." He yelled and looked over at his truck. The police radar was going off; he quickly got into his truck with Nelson and peeled off. Travis and Reggie took out the stop sign, threw it behind some bushes, jumped into the Cutlass, sped off into a long driveway and pulled over next to Bruce where they were out of plain sight. Moments later, a police officer drove by and parked next to the stop sign. The berries and cherries were flashing; the five of them army crawled near the creek and ducked down to watch the two police officers get out of their vehicle. Bruce got his binoculars out from his breast pocket and zoomed in. One of the police officers pulled out his flashlight and followed the trail of blood leading to the deer. He flashed the light in another direction and saw a piece of Aaron's bumper laying on the side of the road. The other officer pulled out his radio as he walked back towards the squad car.

"10-54. We got a possible hit and run. Looks like a deer was struck within the last hour and we got a piece of the vehicle that was most likely involved," the second officer said as he motioned for the other police officer to come towards him. The five of them watched in panic as one of the officers knelt down by the creek. Complete silence. Only the crickets that were chirping about how much fruit and insects they had for the day. A few of the crickets had admitted to cannibalism.

"Welp, glad that the RFD worked. Just a shame that the punks stole a stop sign. We won't be able to get this replaced until tomorrow afternoon. We're probably going to need to have a traffic cop stationed here in the morning." One of the police officers scanned the sign—it showed the location of where it was previously placed.

"I wonder why they just ditched it here," the other one asked.

"Probably saw the news segment or the sticker on the back. I asked the lieutenant to keep the 'Be Real. Don't Steal' initiative on the down low until we caught someone first hand. He insisted that the public had to know right away."

"Yeah, I suppose it helps with making residents more vigilant of the missing signs so they can report them."

"True. But, one day of testing it unannounced would have caught these rat bastards. They steal a sign and kill a deer with no care in the world. We weren't that bad as kids, were we?"

"Much worse these days with all the technology they are exposed to."

"Jesus, so much blood on this bumper from that poor deer. "You think we can get any leads with it?"

"Doubtful, but we can always collect the make and model from it and check the database to be certain."

"Close fucking call," Bruce said under his breath. "If I didn't run into you guys, they would have tracked you down tonight for sure."

"Thanks bro," Aaron replied giving him a fist pound. They all let out a sigh of relief after the police officers put the stop sign in the trunk and drove off slowly patrolling the area.

"We'll get one in Edgewater tomorrow and then call our collection complete," Travis said and tossed a beer to everyone.

"You fuckers are nuts," Nelson replied leaning against Bruce's truck.

"You want to pay for a car wash tomorrow, chump?" Bruce held his beer to his mouth. Nelson raised his eyebrows and looked over at him confused. "I'm just teasing, fucker!" Bruce laughed taking a swig.

They all gazed at the October Hunter's Moon glistening over the creek as they sipped away on fresh crisp PBRs.

"You think we're going to state?" Travis asked the group sitting on the ground scratching his legs.

"We have to. It's destiny. We got the whole core back together just in time," Reggie exclaimed.

"Yeah, as long as you shitheads keep making those big plays." Bruce was chewing on a toothpick and was preparing for another dip of chew.

"Man, we're going to tear shit up next Friday night against Willow Woods," Aaron said confidently raising the beer over his mouth and dumping it in. He gargled it in his mouth for five seconds. "Ahhh, nothing like the fresh mint of Pabts' in the evening."

"Can we get Lyme disease out here?" Nelson suddenly asked and they all looked over at him shaking their heads laughing.

"Only you would get chickenpox senior year in high school," Reggie barked back laughing.

"That shit sucked. I had it for like three weeks back in grade school. I couldn't get out of bed and had a massive headache." Nelson looked around for ticks on the tree he was leaning against. The others ignored him and gave no sympathy for his previous illness.

"You know, fellas, I've been thinking… I think this is my last ride for high school sports. I think I'm going to pass up on baseball this season and just focus on lifting and conditioning. I don't have a shot at collegiate baseball, it's almost fucking impossible." Bruce leaned over and spit chew on the ground. Aaron stopped gazzing at the moon and flashed a puzzled frown at him.

"You're fucking kidding dude, right?"

"Nah, man. I don't care if I am the starting catcher. Our team is a joke and we barely win five-ball games every year. Plus Coach Edwards is taking the head coaching spot and I don't want to deal with him anymore. The ladies will be prime time getting ready for college, if you know what a mean!" Bruce laughed and put his right finger into a circle he made with his left hand imitating intercourse; he made bed squeaking noises.

"Ha-ha, that's true about the chicks. But you are like seven home runs away from the school record, right?" Aaron replied.

"Yeah, but if we wrap up a football state championship I'll be more than satisfied. We can just play home run derby in my parent's backyard like the good ol' days."

"Let's roll, boys. We can catch up during lunch on Monday. I got senior pictures to take tomorrow," Travis said hopping into the Cutlass.

"Ha, you clown. You're going to look like total shit," Reggie laughed slamming the rest of his beer and threw it in the woods. A raccoon jumped out of a tree where the beer can was thrown—they all panicked, jumped into their cars and called it an evening. As they drove off in different directions, Bruce texted them wondering about the police scanner. Although they didn't say it out loud to each other, the three boys knew they had escaped another death sentence. A sound of a venomous snake was above them sizzling away in the clouds. Cat heaven was looking down on them hissing, wondering how they managed to get more than nine lives.

CHAPTER 12

Monday came with a fog—not only in the clouds but also in their brains. The boys were dazed, confused and anxious for the week to come to an end so they could march down the field to compete in the playoffs. The football team sat at their regular tables with their girlfriends and gossiped about what legendary stories happened over the weekend: who bagged the fastest at the local Piggly Wiggly grocery store to increase their hourly wage, who ran through cemeteries to hide out from a successful robbery, who coaxed a girl to use whipped cream and strawberries while losing her virginity, and who fell down a staircase and had to go to the hospital for surgery. Mondays and Fridays were always the rowdiest during the lunch hour.

Suddenly, someone screamed at the top of the grand staircase "Fore!" While holding a golf club high above his head. It was Chad, another class clown who was always involved in senior pranks. He was a short nerdy dude with long hair, freckles and a rat tail; he was popular because he knew how to make everyone laugh. He would come to school with different hair every week, it was a tradition he instilled in the high-school soccer team. There were three other soccer players with him: one was sporting a perfectly shaved eagle in their hair, another had their hair styled with a beer can be poured into a red solo cup, and another had dreadlocks sporting the school colors—blue, white and silver. And then finally, Toby had his long hair pulled over and tied it over his mouth as if the hair on his head was a mustache.

"I love these bastards, these guys are hilarious. They are the World Cup of our campus." Aaron smiled, took a bite of his lasagna and watched the top of the stairs.

The four soccer players pointed their golf clubs in the air towards the cafeteria below them and swung at cardboard boxes beneath them. The cardboard boxes ripped open and thousands of bouncy balls hipped and hopped down the staircase in between the hundreds of students. Everyone roared with laughter and screamed in delight as Chad and his three friends ran down the hallway after the spill. Students frantically started collected the bouncy balls and threw them at each other trying to bounce them off the ground as hard as they could. Bounce! Bounce! Bounce! The balls sailed up, touched the ceiling and rolled across chicken sandwiches, leftover pizza, mediterranean salads and bowls of chili. It was a rainbow of chaos… Red, orange, yellow, smiley face, patriot, multi-colored balls were flying around the cafeteria. Chad appeared again and opened the doors of the gymnasium—the students ran to see what they were doing inside.

A water park had been built inside the school gym. Chad and his three teammates were sliding down a slip and slide linked to a hose that had been connected to a sprout outside and brought into the gym. They had small mini pools set up; they were doing backflips and cannonballs. The rest of the students outside the gym watched in shock as they put on this magnificent water show; right on the same floor they played H.O.R.S.E, capture the football, pickleball and volleyball. They then started to pull out roller paper, threw it to each other from bleacher to bleacher and then threw grenade water balloons. The faculty was struggling to get past the stampede of students watching right by the entrance. Some of the students had gotten so jealous of the ordeal that they got involved and someone yelled "WATER BALLOON BRAWL!"

Water splashed everywhere and Chad picked up the hose and started soaking everyone in his vicinity. His soccer teammates pulled out soaper soakers and started to chase freshmen around the gym. Everyone was falling and slipping over like it was an ice rink, but they didn't have a care in the world. It was the best senior prank anyone had ever pulled on their campus. After three minutes, faculty members were finally able to get in and they blew their whistles. Coach Edwards came out of his office and chased after the four soccer players outside. Janitors quickly piled into the gym turning off the water and mopping the floor down with whatever supplies they could find. Any student involved in participating in the water balloon brawl was detained and taken to the principal's office.

Mr. Swanson, the principal of the school (and the father of Rebecca Swanson) was not available as he had to leave for a family emergency. The assistant principal ordered Chad and his three teammates to be expelled for the rest of the semester and would have to make up classes in the final semester or have to wait to graduate after completing summer courses if they didn't have enough credits. Everyone else was given a two-week suspension from school. Gym class was suspended indefinitely and the athletic director was already looking to reserve the middle school for the opening games for the high school basketball and volleyball season.

"That was the most fucking epic thing I have ever seen," Reggie bellowed holding his hands on top of his head in joy walking down the hall with Travis and Reggie.

"Chad is a bad bad badass mother fucker. He's probably not going to be back in class for a while though." Travis put a piece of Wrigley Juicy Fruit gum in his mouth. Angela was by her locker and had a pissed-off face.

"Why didn't you text me back last night? You said you were coming over to my parents' house for dinner," Angela barked at him holding her textbook against her chest.

"Sorry, babe. I passed out watching football after my senior photos. I was on the couch all day and passed out like a baby." Travis winked at her.

"Shut the fuck up, Travis. My mom was going to surprise us with free tickets to a concert in the park last night. She spent like thirty bucks on each of them." Angela punched him on the shoulder as hard as she could; Travis held onto it and winced in pain. Aaron and Reggie covered their mouths to hold in their giggling and Travis responded by flipping them the bird.

"Fuck, I'm sorry Angela. I'll pay your mom back, I swear," Travis said softly as he continued to hold his pulsating shoulder. Angela gave him the cold shoulder and walked into her psychology class with Travis following her.

"Ughhh hmmmmm, Mr. Connery. It's not the ninth hour just yet. I think you're in calculus after lunch, sir," Mr. Davis, the psychology teacher said clearing his throat, raising his glasses and looking at his watch. Travis stared at Angela; she

gave him the "throat slit" neck signal and opened her textbook.
Travis threw his hands up in the air agitated and let out a huge
groan as Mr. Davis shut the door behind him. The intermission
bell rang and they all went their separate ways to their class
after lunch. Down below on the main floor of the school,
squishy noises of the janitor's shoes could be heard; they were
cleaning up the aftermath of Hurricane Chad, a category 5 that
caused twenty-five casualties (the number of students
suspended) and the estimated damage was damn near $50,000.

***

It was now the ninth hour and Aaron sat back in his chair in
science class with Mrs. Gleason. He couldn't stop laughing
from seeing Travis get humiliated by his girlfriend and the
hilarious water show he had seen a few hours prior. Mrs.
Gleason had her hair up in a ponytail and smiled back at him.
She had thanked him several times for acting as a guard
towards her home during "Fuck the Faculty" week and even
gave him a $20.00 gift certificate to Grill & Chill, a fan-
favorite gourmet burger restaurant a few blocks from his house.
Today, they were passing out the results of the physics exam he
took last week. He picked up the paper and glanced at it several
times. How could this be? A perfect A+ with a red marker was
at the top corner of his exam. He flipped through the four pages

and there was no mark of any error. It was the first exam he had aced of the semester; he stared back at Mrs. Gleason and returned a smile with two thumbs up. Was this another thank you for the protection services he offered a few weeks ago? He turned behind him where Rebecca would usually sit to ask what she got on the exam, but she wasn't there. The rumor was that she was pregnant, reason why her father had left for a family emergency earlier in the day. It wouldn't have been a surprise—she probably had hooked up with forty different students in her tenure. *She was due to get prego and have a little Donovan or Shelby*, according to Aaron. Aaron was relieved it wasn't him—being a father would've definitely prevented him from playing college football. That was a fact. Another fact? One hundred percent of the male students who slept with her probably screamed in agony when they shot hot dragon fire piss from their peckers whenever they went to the bathroom. Clap On! Clap off. Nope, this wasn't as easy as turning off a lightbulb. "The Clap" needed some antibiotic treatment to stop that burn.

Class was dismissed for the day and students ran to their lockers to grab their backpacks and go attend practice, watch their favorite after-school television shows, or go to work at the local grocery store and fast food joints. Aaron stayed in his seat while Mrs. Gleason wiped the marker of her lesson off the whiteboard. He let out a smile as her sexy buttocks shook back and forth while erasing away letters from the periodic table. The eleven elements necessary for human life: oxygen, carbon, hydrogen, nitrogen, calcium, phosphorus, potassium, sulfur, sodium, chlorine and magnesium were all bubbling inside his body like lava in a hot volcano eruptions. Mrs. Gleason turned around and saw Aaron sitting at his desk staring directly at her. Good thing she couldn't see beneath his desk in the crotch of his jeans.

"Aaron, can I help you with something? What's the matter?"She picked up her water bottle and took a huge swig inviting him to speak.

"Why'd you do it? You didn't have to," Aaron replied picking away at his ear.

"Excuse me?'

"The exam. An A+. I didn't deserve that."

"Huh? Are you implying that I just handed you a perfect score?"

"Well, yeah kinda," Aaron shrugged and tried to press his raging erection down so he could stand up.

"Aaron, I was seriously in shock and very impressed when I graded your exam. You have come a long way over the past months. You were the only one that got a perfect score. As much as I appreciate what you did for me, I'm not going to do any favors when it comes to academics. I'm an honest teacher and I thought the gift certificate was more than satisfactory."

Aaron's boner pocket rocket was still ready for lift-off and he stood up walking over to her. "How about one more favor?" Aaron asked softly as he stood glaring into her eyes.

"Yes?"

Aaron went in for a smooch. She shrieked and slapped him right across the face. Aaron let out a smile and nodded his head.

"Thank you, that's exactly what I wanted. A snap back to reality because I truly don't know what to believe anymore," he said walking over to grab his backpack. She snapped her fingers and pointed towards the door. Aaron laughed and folded his aced exam to put it in his pocket. "I'm truly really sorry, but it was a double-dog dare that started four years ago."

"Uh huh. Now we're officially even. Get out of my classroom, asshole," she said while crossing her arms and standing behind her desk. Aaron walked out, closed the door behind him and Mrs. Gleason blew him a kiss as she rolled her eyes. His jaw dropped; he almost jumped through the roof in joy. He ran down the ghost-town hallways towards the locker room to tell everyone he had finally accomplished his dare. It wasn't as reckless and memorable as Chad's water park extravaganza earlier in the day, but it was the only senior prank he was interested in partaking in. The locker room door was locked; he banged on it for several minutes fearing he'd be late for practice. After about a minute of waiting at the door, he looked down and saw a piece of yellow paper laying on the ground that had been initially taped to the door. "PRACTICE Canceled TODAY AND TOMORROW. WILL RESUME WEDNESDAY. THX, COACH EDWARDS ."

Aaron stood at the piece of paper confused like a lost abandoned puppy left for dead on the side of the road in a cardboard box. It was less than a week from the playoffs, why in the world would football practice be canceled? The game was this coming Friday evening. How would two days be enough time to prepare for Willow Woods? He let out a sigh and walked out the door; he took out his phone and noticed he had eight text messages and twelve missed phone calls. They were from Reggie, Travis and Bruce. The lost puppy trapped inside him walked outside in the now blaring hot October afternoon and vertigo set in rapidly.

CHAPTER 13

Aaron looked out into the parking lot and saw local media and police storming the area asking students questions. He walked with his hands in his pockets towards his Cutlass and started to open the door. Smack! Someone had hit him hard in the shoulder.

"Ow! What the fucking hell?" Aaron turned around holding up his fists to deliver a pounce in return. It was Travis with Reggie and Bruce behind them. They all had tears in their eyes.

"Where the fuck were you, dude!" Reggie cried trying to hold back his tears.

"What, what, what, what!" Aaron fired back demanding an answer.

"Rebecca... She's dead, man. She's fucking dead!" Bruce whispered in a high pitch as a tear slowly dropped down his cheek. Aaron watched the tear fall to the ground and stumbled backward into his car. Goosebumps pulsated through his body and he tried to fight back the tears himself. He glanced at the three of them shifting back at their faces in silence. He didn't have to ask how she died based on their reaction. He knew he was somehow responsible.

"What the fuck are we going to do!" Bruce screamed tearing up and covering his face. Aaron thought it was so very odd to see him in this state. He was always known as the tough guy that didn't take shit from anyone.

"We tried calling Nelson and he isn't returning our calls. He was there too." Reggie sobbed.

They all turned over to the "Silver Eagle Atrium" which was a mini corridor near the entrance of the school. It consisted of benches, student art, names of notable alumni engraved into the sidewalk and a statue of the Silver Eagle next to the American flag and the school flag. Usually, there were food trucks that were permitted to sell healthy food options like salads, vegan sandwiches and smoothies. But not today. Instead, there were students mourning the death of Rebecca Swanson, the beautiful young daughter of Principal Swanson. Students were setting up a vigil, writing their favorite memories on a collage. School and all sports activities were to be canceled for the next two days. Ordinary school wouldn't be canceled for a death of a student, but because it was the principal's daughter, it became necessary for administration needs.

The four of them stood close to the Cutlass like it was their fortress, only protection from this murderous vortex each of them contributed to. They watched in horror as close friends of Rebecca held hands and bowed their heads as they prayed in silence. They overheard some of the outcasts that were often picked on by Rebecca make a mockery of the whole ordeal.

"That bitch got what she deserved," a dorky boy muttered walking past the four boys in the parking lot. He crouched down and picked up a piece of trash that looked to be a soggy old bar coaster and stuffed it in the pocket of his khaki shorts. "Can't stand damn litterers."

"I mean, maybe a disremembered face she had to live with forever…. But death? Maybe that's too harsh," a dorky girl said touching the tips of her glasses.

"Maybe you don't remember prom last year when she pantsed me and my dick was exposed to the whole school," he replied taking a swig from a bottle of Vitamin Water and holding his crotch. "I didn't know dudes were supposed to shave down there at that point either. Now, I'm stuck with 'Joey The Fro Bro Show' until I finally get out of here," Joey said.

"Yes, that was an awful night. I'm sorry, but," the girl dork said covering her mouth trying to hold back her laughter.

"Shut the fuck up, Kathy, otherwise I'll wish you dead too," Joey yelled. He now noticed that his response was rather loud and that others may have noticed. Kathy let out a gasp and he took her by the hand; they trotted to his car and they took off down the street in a hurry.

"Well, what the fuck are we going to do?" Aaron asked wiping tears from his eyes.

"Well, maybe we can pin it on Joey. You heard what he just said," Bruce sad sporting an angry frown.

"Yes, how the hell do we know he wasn't involved in her death anyway? He was the one that she always picked on… wet willies, pantsing, dumping used tampons from the girls' trash can on him and then pretending to make it up to him by asking him out," Reggie exclaimed. Travis raised his eyebrows, spit a loogie and stared into Reggie's eyes.

"So, how do we do it? Perhaps we make Joey's hit lit with her name on it?" Travis asked.

"Fuck that, we're not framing him. He didn't deserve all that shit just for trying to kiss her back in grade school. And quite frankly, he doesn't deserve to rot in jail for something he didn't do. You must be fucking stupid if you really think others will believe Rebecca was riding shotgun with Joey. Plus, isn't his dad a police officer?" Aaron darted back putting his face in his hands. Everyone then stood in silence and saw Mrs. Gleason by the door sobbing with a gut-wrenching evil stare.

"Why is she fucking looking at us like that?" Bruce whispered.

"Because I just tried pulling a 'Joey on Rebecca' and tried to kiss her, and she is probably the same shock we're dealing with." Aaron sighed. None of his friends questioned his remark. They knew it to be true, but there was no point for praise or congratulating him for accomplishing his one and only senior prank. The four of them had fear of being in orange jumpsuits locked behind cells for life planted into their rotting skulls. They watched in silence as Mrs. Gleason turned and walked towards the faculty parking lot.

"Okay, okay, I think we were all joking about framing Joey. But we can't stick around here arguing about what we need to do." Travis slammed his hand on the back of the car. Aaron looked at him sharply throwing his hands up because of the antenna he had just snapped in two.

Aaron had just repaired the Cutlass from the deer strike and the very next something else goes to shit. "Sorry dude, I'll fix it once we get this all settled out, Travis sighed and picked up the piece that was on the ground.

"What about Nelson?" Bruce replied. Everyone stared at him like he was the grim reaper.

"Frame fucking Nelson?!" Aaron screamed and pushed Bruce into his car. Bruce threw up his fists in a flash and they were both separated by Reggie and Travis.

"No, you fucking dumbass. He's my best friend. I mean, he has to be involved so we all have the same story, you stupid piece of shit. You'll be sorry if you ever touch me again. Remember, Rodge Clement," Bruce scolded. Now he really was the grim reaper. His pupils were vibrating out of his eyes sockets; he was sweating profusely and his eyebrows flared in the abnormal sizzling hot October inferno. He grabbed his chew from the breast pocket without leaving an eye on Aaron.

The short tall tale of Rodge Clements. Back in sophomore year, Rodge used to be a hotshot. He had Daddy's money for a nice green Ford Mustang, all the nice cologne he wanted due to his mother owning a fragrance store… and he would never be turned down for a date. One time, he took it a little too far. He went up to Bruce and his girlfriend at the time Gaby, and asked her out on a date. Gaby let out a gasp and said "Yes." She was obligated to. No one could dodge Rodge Clements. But that day Bruce decided the streak was over. Later that afternoon, Bruce was on the shitter after having two cheeseburgers and cheese fries; he heard Rodge walk in to go the sink. It was his normal routine to brush, flush and shave after lunch. If anyone else did it, others would think they were crazy, but because it was Roger everyone would bat an eye. His father was a big shot architect in the city and had donated his wealth all across the community. It helped the high-school sports teams, the homeless, the mentally challenged. A little bit of everything.

Bruce, for the most part, had a post-lunch crap routine himself. He officially ended his relationship with Gaby in front of other football players, making it look like he was the one who dumped Gaby instead of her leaving for Rodge. It appeared that Rodge was just joking when he asked her anyway. Bruce got some hoots and hollers from his friends for ending the relationship, while Gaby ran down the hallway bawling her eyes out. Bruce didn't chase after her. The cheeseburgers chased inside his intestines. He peered through the crack in the stall door and watched Rodge brush away his squeaky clean white teeth as he whistled with his electric toothbrush. Rodge turned to his mouth wash and started to gargle.

Bruce swung the unflushed stall door and grabbed Rodge by the back of the collar. He gave him a punch to the stomach which caused an eruption of mouthwash to cover the mirror. Rodge let out a groan and tried to scream for help, but Brush covered his mouth and brought him into the stall.

"I'll help you finish with the flossing this time around. Free of charge." Bruce screamed as he dumped Rodge's head into the toilet filled with a steamy quadruple log pile of shit. Bruce pulled him up as Rodge tried to plug his nose from the disgusting aroma blanketing his nostrils. Bruce swiped his arm away from his nose, dunked his head in a few more times and then gave him a swirly. Rodge had smears of crap all over his face. Bruce dragged him out of the stall door and threw him out the bathroom door where he fell on the ground and rolled to his side coughing and spitting out shit toilet water. The bell rang as students started coming down the hallways. Bruce stood over Rodge who let out a shriek and Bruce planted him with a loogie filled with chew right in the face. He then held up a roll of toilet paper over his head and dropped it on his face. Just like a patented mic drop.

"Don't fuck with the Loose Cannon Bruce Shannon!" He screamed as two-hundred jaws dropped to the floor. There still was a small shit stain on the tile floor that wouldn't get replaced until the school was torn down. Either the janitors were too scared to touch it—it was validation that no one was ever to fuck with Bruce. After that day, the Clements reputation went from gold to shit. Their family packed up, left the town and started over somewhere in Europe. Bruce's family reputation went from shit to gold. Bruce's self-proclaimed nickname lived on and he was known for being the badass mother fucker on campus. He was suspended for two weeks but his father couldn't have been prouder. The day helped save Bruce father's company from the competition from the Clements. When you can host parties at an unsupervised mansion, you become a walking legend.

"Sorry, Bruce. I just don't know what reality is anymore. Won't happen again. We gotta all fight through this together," Aaron said softly walking towards Bruce. Bruce let out a subtle shrug and gave him a fist pump to signal a truce between them.

"Okay, let's go pick up Nelson and head to my parent's cabin for the next two days to sort this out. We're not doing any good discussing it here," Travis said. They all agreed, got in their cars and drove out of the school parking lot as they glanced in sorrow at the students who were continuing to pray, light candles, place flowers and share memories on portraits of Rebecca Lynn Swanson.

As they left the parking lot, a Channel 7 NEWS media van passed them on their way to tell a story about the tragic accident and interview students. The only ones that knew the true story were the four of them plus Nelson. At least they hoped so. Nelson was prone to spill the beans on rumors and secrets around campus. You either hated or loved him. He either had dirt on you or could hand you a shovel to lead you to the dirt on someone else. They were hoping he hadn't buried them six feet under in dirt. A little solitude was necessary at this moment and they all drove in a wolf pack down the backroads separately to Nelson's house. Aaron turned on the radio trying to get some peace of mind.

A slow depressing song came on and he set his finger on the dial to turn it, but it was motionless. The lyrics from *Landslide* by Fleetwood Mac immediately made him think of Rebecca's blue eyes, blonde hair, her strut down the school hallways with her gossipy clique, and the night he fled Bruce's party with her. Chills jumped down his spine and he started to ball uncontrollably. Motionless, in a trance and sobbing, he thought about running away forever and never coming back; change his identity and move to another part of the world where he could put this misery all behind them. There were always five options in this scenario: 1. Evasion 2. Persuasion (convincing others they weren't tied to it and living life as normal as they could) 3. Confession (turning themselves in and hoping that his brother would be their lawyer) 4. Falsification (framing others so it looked like they weren't involved with the tragic death). 5. Self-mutilation (just entering into the most depressing state and realizing that neither jail time was inevitable or knowing that if they got away with it that the guilty conscious would never ween off). He reluctantly decided to follow the vehicles ahead so that the five fugitives could agree on one of the five options. Wiping more tears from his eyes, he finally flipped the station.

"Good evening, this is Charlotte Dawson for a quick break in the 70's rewind to share some developing news. Sadly, earlier today, it was reported that a senior from Cedar Creek High School was killed in a motor vehicle accident. She was pronounced dead at the scene in the early morning hours. There was a missing stop sign at the intersection of Dunwoody & Damascus that caused the tragedy. A new stop sign was scheduled to be put in the morning hours after the accident has already occurred. There is reason to believe another vehicle may have been involved, but had fled the scene. Another license plate was found fifty yards from the crash. More details will be shared on our 9 PM newscast." Aaron turned off the radio and pulled over on Nelson's street.

They had parked in a Cul-de-sac, one block down from Nelson's—there was some minor road construction happening in the neighborhood. They each took turns trying to contact Nelson, but it went straight to voicemail. Bruce scrolled through his contacts and decided to call Peter, Nelson's younger brother.

"Hello?" Peter picked up and paused the video game he was playing.

"Peter, is your brother home?" Bruce asked as he spit chew out the window. Some of it landed inside his car and he slammed on the dashboard.

"Yeah, he came home from school a bit ago and went to bed. I guess he has food poisoning or something," Peter said taking his glasses off and rubbing his eyes.

"Gotcha. Are your parents home?"

"No, why?"

Click.

Bruce waved the three others to his truck and they decided they needed to urgently wake up Nelson from his good ol' cat nap. As they discussed their game plan, they passed an orange construction work sign—a stick figure man shoveling up the pavement. Aaron stared at it in disgust and wanted to give it a roundhouse kick to the moon. Every road sign they passed let out a roaring demonic high-pitched laughter with snapping jaws. They all wanted payback for their other friends and family that had been stolen around the community.

Ready. Set. Break. The four of them broke from their huddle and awkwardly waved at construction workers as they weaved through the chopped-up sidewalk leading to Nelson's house. Aaron went to the front door and rang the doorbell. Peter opened the door with an ice cream sandwich in his hand and Aaron lied saying that he needed to borrow a baseball glove from Nelson. Peter shrugged, took a bite out of his sandwich and pointed to the basement door. Aaron coaxed him into coming to the basement with him to locate the glove as the other three peaked out the backdoor and waited for the coast to be clear. The three of them slowly crept up to the door and walked into the kitchen. There was a jar filled with licorice on the counter; Bruce opened it up and they all took one for the road up to Nelson's bedroom.

Travis turned the handle but it was locked. They turned and looked at each other as they began to hear movement within the bedroom. Nelson was silently pushing furniture against the door to prevent them from coming in. Bruce slammed his fist on the door, "we know you're in there, we need to fucking talk." Bruce yelled. Nelson continued to stack chairs, dressers, desks and even his bed on top of each other. He frantically searched around the room to see how he could continue to play Tetris against his door.

"Open up, man. Please!" Reggie begged.

"No, I don't want to be involved in this shit. Just go away. I won't tell anyone," Nelson shouted back.

Bruce continued to lower his shoulder into the door, but it wouldn't budge. Nelson continued to shout back pleading for them to stop. He sat on the floor with his legs crossed shaking back and forth violently as a river of tears poured down his face. Travis ran into the door as fast as he could, bounced off and landed near the staircases. He thought he too had a river pouring down his face. Instead, it was blood coming from his nostrils from the nasty fall he had just taken. Blood poured into his hand as he tried to prevent it from landing on the carpet. He went into the bathroom, turned on the light and grabbed a box of Kleenex to try to stop the blood. After he exited, he flipped the light switch off leaving remnants of blood on it.

Aaron was at the bottom of the stairs staying guard for Nelson's parents and younger brother. Bruce continued to lower his shoulder into the door and he was starting to make progress. Nelson screamed at the top of his lungs for help and Peter could hear him from the basement. Peter tried to run up the stairs to see what all the ruckus was, but Aaron put out his leg to trip him. Peter fell face first into a box filled with antiques in the corner of the hallway, and laid motionless on the ground. Aaron tapped him on the face to wake him up from the nasty spill.

Back upstairs, Reggie was getting anxious and decided there had to be another way to get into the room. He walked into Nelson's parent's room. There was dirty laundry everywhere: bras, panties, ties, socks on the bed, and even some clothes in the bathtub. Reggie looked at a picture of Nelson and his family hanging on the wall as he listened to the squeals of Nelson down the hallway. He went over to the nightstand covered with dirty dishes and opened up the window that led to the roof. He crawled on the roof towards Nelson's rooms. Nelson was backing up to the window as he stared at the I, J, L, O, S, T and Z Tetris pieces of furniture puzzle he orchestrated for his protection.

Aaron woke Peter up by wafting another ice cream sandwich over his nose. Peter woke up delighted and took a bite from Aaron's hand. Aaron smiled and convinced Peter they were trying to treat Nelson's food poisoning symptoms with bananas smothered in honey. Peter nodded and understood. The ongoing shrieks of terror made sense. Nelson absolutely despised bananas. Aaron coaxed Peter back downstairs and said he wanted to watch him play video games.

Reggie crawled to Nelson's window and saw him trying to score more points in his game of Tetris. He was now throwing pillows, blankets, clothes, board games, DVDs on top of all his furniture. Travis returned with a screwdriver he found in the garage to pick the lock. Travis twisted the screwdriver and unlocked the door while Reggie tried to pry the window open. Nelson was being attacked from both sides and rolled his head over like an owl perched on a tree. He stared in shock at Reggie kneeling down on the roof. Reggie punched his fist through the window, jumped in and ran to the door to clear it to let everyone in.

"What the fuck is your problem?" Bruce screamed. Nelson started to immediately ball his eyes out.

"I don't want to go to jail. I don't want to go to jail," he muttered slowly, with his back against the wall and dreadfully slid down it onto his ass, sliding towards the floor with his back against the wall "Fuckkkkkkkkk!!!!" He wiped tears from his eyes as he looked up at Bruce, Travis and Reggie who had all been bloodied, beaten and bruised from trying to get into his room.

"That's why we need to fucking talk. We don't want to go to jail either, so we need to make sure our stories are right," Travis explained.

"If you don't come with us, will put you in a straitjacket and take you with us," Reggie barked.

"No, I won't tell anyone. I swear. Just don't mention my name," Nelson pleaded.

Negotiation time was over. The three of them grabbed him and he let out a hideous nightmarish cry. *Boy oh boy, were those bananas as the remedy for his food poison rotten*, Peter paused his video game downstairs and Travis put a blanket over Nelson's face to try to mute the violent screams. Travis noticed masks in Nelson's closet and passed them out to disguise their face; Travis took the gorilla, Reggie the scarecrow, Aaron the mummy and Bruce the clown. They all carried Nelson down the stairs and snuck him outside. As they snuck around the backyards, one of the construction workers who was on a cigarette break noticed the boys running through the woods. He noticed a white sneaker flailing back and forth underneath the blanket the four boys were carrying and blew out smoke. He turned to another worker sitting on the curb talking on the phone.

"Hey Eddie, you gotta see this shit. I just witnessed an abduction," he said.

Eddie ended his phone call, walked over to him and peered through the wooded area for a long three seconds. Nothing. They had vanished. He turned to the other construction worker and smacked his lips. "I thought your knee was finally all healed up."

"Huh?"

"Quit taking oxycodone, you're acting like you're a medium again seeing ghosts and shit."

Nelson was thrown in the front seat of Bruce's truck. Travis hopped in the backseat and handed Reggie the keys to his SUV. Travis wanted to be with Nelson to ensure he didn't squeal and also wanted to ensure that everyone had access to his vehicle since it was the most spacious. The plan for the game of musical cars was: Bruce would drive his truck with Nelson and Travis, Reggie would drop off his car, Aaron would pick up Reggie with his car and drive back to Travis's SUV, Reggie would drive Travis's SUV and follow Aaron back to his house to drop off his car, and then meet the others at Travis parents' cabin to hash out the details to save their future from being bulldozed into oblivion.

***

Before Reggie and Aaron could make their way out to the cabin, they had one final task. They drove over to Aaron's house and parked in the backyard next to the treehouse. They were careful not to drive over the grass as Aaron's father had just mowed the lawn for the last time of the season. On the last day of lawn mowing for the year, it had always been a family tradition to drink Moonshine and eat shepherd's pie. Aaron unlocked the treehouse and covered his nose as the potent aroma of gasoline lingered inside. He shined the flashlight on his phone, noticed a red fuel tank and a weed wacker leaning against the wall.

"Oh shit, oh shit, my dad was in here," Aaron said putting his hands on his head trying to prevent it from exploding into a bubble of guilt.

"Son of a bitch!" Reggie yelled as he shined his flashlight on its weed wacker. He turned over to the quilts covering the signs and peaked underneath them. Phew! The signs were still there just how they left them.

"I'm hoping he didn't see that shit," Aaron said.

"It doesn't look like he did. Plus, he would have called you right away, right?" Reggie asked confidently.

"Yeah, definitely."

Aaron climbed out of the treehouse and pushed the backseat of the car. They created an assembly line to work together to quickly load the signs into the back of the Travis' Kia Sorento. All nine signs were still intact: Dead End, Deer Crossing, 55 MPH, Railroad Crossing, Yield, Do Not Enter, No Parking, Road Work Ahead and Reserved Parking.

Aaron got back into the driver's seat and Reggie patted his hands together to get the dust and cobwebs off. They started driving off the street and Aaron's dad chased them down the street like a mad man waving his arms up in the air yelling for them to stop.

"Fucking GO GO GO!" Reggie screamed looking back at Aaron's dad who was still dressed in a business suit and dress shoes.

"I can't! He'll just call me to come home if I don't stop now." Aaron squealed like a pig under pressure grasping the wheel and profusely sweating from his forehead. Too much anxiety had clouded their heads over the past few weeks.

Aaron's vision was becoming blurry due to the stress and he pulled over.

"What if he saw it? What if he saw the signs?" Reggie bellowed and smacked Aaron on the shoulder encouraging him to speed off.

"Don't fucking hit me again," Aaron snapped back. Reggie crossed his arms and sat staring in the rearview mirror as Aaron's dad approached them.

"Hey guys!" Aaron's dad shouted placing his hands on the roof of the car on the passenger side. "Why do you have Travis' car?"

"Reggie ran out of gas so we borrowed it quick." Aaron lied.

"You guys are really getting on my nerves. Why do you all constantly wait for the fuel tank below E before you decide that a car needs gas to run from point A to point B? Why'd you guys drive down this way? The gas station is back near Dunwoody." Aaron's dad shouted throwing his arms in the air with disappointment.

Now Aaron thought they were being interrogated and sweat a bit more.

"We're playing musical cars, just needed to make sure Aaron's car had been dropped off back here," Reggie quickly replied.

"Whatever you guys say. Remember there is a curfew for the rest of the week. 9PM. So make sure you get your asses home by then," Aaron's dad said with a look of suspicion stamped on his face.

"Yes, Dad."

"Are you sure you guys don't want to stop in for shepherd's pie? I'll even let you sample the Moonshine if you promise to stay in. All of you guys were over for last year's dinner to celebrate the real welcoming of fall. No more yard work, except a little racking here and there. Tyler is still here too."

"No thanks, we have to get the car back to Travis anyway," Reggie said.

Aaron's dad shrugged disappointed that his son and friends weren't participating in the tradition and waved them goodbye. Aaron immediately returned the favor by giving a strike back to Reggie's shoulder.

"What the fuck, dude? We're free," Reggie moaned.

"Sure, but that doesn't mean you get free shots on me," Aaron said.

CHAPTER 14

As they began to exit the city to decipher the chaotic puzzle they had to solve, they witnessed something that would be the most gut-wrenching scene they could handle at that time: a tall slender crossguard was directing children and their parents across the street from a park. Instilled with paralyzing goosebumps, the crossguard flashed the big bright red stop sign he was holding right in front of their car. The stop sign hissed violently like a snake and tried to attack them with its menacing eyes. Aaron put the car in park, slid down his seat and let out a scream of terror. Reggie shook his head in disbelief and he violently chewed his nails as tears dropped down his face. They were the victims of their own horror story they created, but only they knew they were the suspects. They felt disgusted and began to panic uncontrollably as they feared the most severe consequences imaginable.

Aaron and Reggie pulled up to a gas station out of town and filled up for the hour drive up to Travis parents' cabin. While Reggie was fueling, Aaron used his fake ID to get a few cases of beer. They drove in silence sipping down road beers with oldies on the radio. Mourning the death of Rebecca.

Grieving the demise of scholarships. Grieving the loss of potential friendships.

It was now 7 PM. The sun had called it a day and tucked in for the night with its teddy bear. The moon danced above their heads, the frogs gave their final growls and the owls hooted in delight at the constellations in the darkening sky. Aaron and Reggie drove up a long gravel driveway and passed a large oak tree with a tire swing, a trailer and a large bonfire they could spot in the backyard.

The cabin was built back in 1932 on ten acres of land and was still alive and kicking. It had been passed on from Travis's grandparents to his own and it would eventually be passed onto Travis once his parents retired and moved down to Florida. At some point, Travis wanted to utilize some of the property for farming and hunting, and build out additional homes and rent it out for vacationers. It was right on Lake Sabathia —the dock was equipped with a speed boat, fishing boat and three jet skis. Unfortunately, it'd be too damn cold to use the toys for this trip and all of the dopamine had been flushed from their bodies to even want to consider taking the boats out for a cruise.

***

Inside the cabin, taxidermy coated the walls from all the successful family hunting trips from Montana and Wyoming. There were five bedrooms, three bathrooms, an outdoor pool, an indoor hot tub, and a gaming room with a pool table, billiards and a humidor. They all had their own bedroom for the evening, but they collectively agreed to sleep in the living room because they were scared shitless of a possible return of Rebecca that would haunt their visit to the cabin to STOP them from progressing further with their lives. The funeral was planned for Saturday, six days away. They couldn't phantom making an appearance to see her lie lifeless in a coffin.

Aaron and Reggie parked next to Bruce's truck and walked over to distribute beer to the other three, who were sitting in silence on a picnic table next to the bonfire. The other three and Bruce looked up, thanked for the beer and spit chew into the fire. They opened their beers and walked over to the back of Travis' SUV where they started to unload the signs from the car. One by one, they tossed them into the fire and watched them go up in flames. Nelson had calmed down from earlier in the day and realized he had been an accomplice; it was vital that they stuck together if they were ever questioned by police.

"Pockets full of posies," Nelson muttered squinting his eyes from the smoke and taking a drink of beer.

"Ashes, ashes," Bruce replied staring into the fire.

"We all WON'T fall down," Aaron stated and poured more gasoline into the fire while staring into their eyes like he would when it was the final ticks of a football game and he was calling the play. They all nodded in agreement.

"What's that?" Nelson pointed at the fire and jumped back nearly falling over a rack they were using to brush ashes back into the pit.

"What the fuck are you talking about?" Bruce took a sip of his beer and peered into the fire. He got down on his knees and let out a big cough as smoke filled his lungs.

"No fucking way!" Reggie screamed in dismay as he too looked at the sign.

Their five hearts were racing at fifty-five miles per hour as they examined the back of the 55 MPH sign that was glancing back at them and giving a "fuck you, we gotcha." The sticker was glaring at their eyes, which looked to be one of the RFD signs that the police officers installed on several of the community street signs.

"Shit, shit, shit" Aaron muttered as sweat dripped from his forehead.

Travis didn't say a word, got closer to the fire and stared directly at the sign. He lifted up the rake, tossed the sign over onto the grass and poured beer on top of it to get a better look.

"Looks like a reflector sticker, but we better be safe than sorry. Let's ditch this one back into town," Travis said.

"How do we know that they all don't have one?" Nelson asked.

"How do we know that they don't all have one?" Travis mocked back. "Pick up the rake and check yourself." Nelson grabbed it from Travis and brushed all the signs over to see if he could identify any other potential RFD chips implanted. All the others looked on peering over the fire shielding themselves from the smoke as they took sips of their beer.

"Okay, okay, it looks fine." Nelson sighed and dropped the rake.

"Good, now I think in order for you to prove you won't go chicken shit on us, you have to be the one to ditch it in town," Reggie said looking for approval from others.

"Yeah, Nelson, I agree. This way we can officially make a pact." Aaron pleaded.

"What? No. I'll get caught right away. I'm not doing that shit. Please. This isn't fucking fair," Nelson begged.

"Come on kid, you'll be fine. It will take you ten fucking minutes," Travis said as he took the keys from his back pocket to his SUV and handed it to Nelson who refused to take them.

"This is horse shit. Someone has to come with me at least. Come on," Nelson begged again.

"No man, you have to do this on your own. Trust me, you are going to be okay. I'm only agreeing with this so we know everyone is in this together," Bruce said staring into the fire.

"Fucking fine," Nelson bellowed snatching the keys from Travis and marched away.

"Forgetting something, dude?" Aaron asked pointing at the 55 MPH sign. A tear rolled down Nelson's cheek and he dragged the sign with his foot to avoid being burnt.

"Jesus man, don't be a pussy," Bruce belched, picked up the sign and threw it in the back of the trunk for Nelson. Bruce returned to the fire moments later as Nelson drove down the driveway balling his eyes out.

"It's for his own good," Travis said pouring more gasoline on the fire to aid in expediting the engulfment of evidence.

"Yeah, I feel bad for the kid. He was pleading for me to come with him back there," Bruce took out his chew for another dip.

"I highly doubt there was an RFD on that sign. We took that sign way before the fuzz started to get involved," Travis replied.

"The fuzz?" Reggie asked.

"Ya, some 60s shit slang for the cops or something," Travis said as he went back to smashing the signs into more pieces with a shovel.

Nelson returned twenty minutes later and walked back into the backyard with the top of his shirt douched in water.

"Fuck dude, you're going to die from dehydration from all that balling you did." Bruce pointed at his shirt.

"It's not fucking tears, asshole," Nelson snapped back. "It's from a creek that I fell in. The current is strong and it made the sign go westward."

"Nice dude, nice fucking work. I knew you'd handle it like a champ," Travis said patting him on the back.

"Thanks!" Nelson glared back at Bruce for insulting him.

"So… what do we now?" Aaron stared up into the darkening sky.

"Let's wait until tomorrow to talk shop. I know it's sickening to try to enjoy ourselves after what happened today, but I'd rather try to just chill and drink some beers with you guys and wait until the morning," Travis said convincingly.

"Agreed," the other four said in unison staring into fire mesmerized. Their lips were zipped shut for the remainder of the evening. They just wanted each other's company and comfort through this wild rollercoaster they'd be riding over the next few weeks. They burped, farted, coughed and drank their two packs of PBR's. They smoked cigars staring into the fire and glanced around staring at each other trapped within their own solitude. Meditation for their mental bruise and medication supplied by plentiful booze.

Buzzed up, they decided to call it a night and put out the fire. Aaron handed everyone a glass of water so they could try to avoid a hangover and think straight for their game plan powwow in the morning. They had two more days to hash out the details and make a pact to take all these signs of deception to the grave and never speak of the tragedy again. When they'd go back to reality, they would have football practice on Thursday and a playoff game on Saturday. They knew it would be a challenge to get through, but figured it'd take a few months to fully recover from the agonizing mental agony they were all dealing with. Travis and Bruce claimed the sofa bed, Aaron sprawled out in the love seat as best as he could, Reggie rested in the recliner and Nelson curled up in a ball down on the floor with two blankets and two fluffy pillows. He got the shaft, so they tried to accommodate him with the best quality of sleeping gear. All of the five beds in the cabin remained vacant —no one could sleep alone.

Aaron tossed and turned throughout the night experiencing horrific nightmares. He was naked being lowered on a rope from a military helicopter and beneath his feet was pitch black darkness. Aaron wanted to plug his ears—it was so loud from the humming of the helicopter blades chopping away at the sunset glistening above him. If he used his hands to plug his ears, he could've lost hold of the rope. A man with sunglasses and a green mohawk was driving the helicopter and gave him a thumbs up, signaling that he was going to release him. Aaron screamed and fell deep inside the black hole of darkness. Now, stuck inside a snow globe, he looked up and saw someone outside of the globe bending over to watch him. The snow globe was a maze in itself and the walls were filled with white and black zebra patterns. He roamed around trying to escape as he was blanketed with snow. Crunch, crunch, crunch. His feet slowly made their way through the deep foot of snow. Frostbite trickled up his entire body and he shivered violently while begging for the face looking down at him. He waved his hands to get attention, but the face simply smiled back and laughed. The face blew into the snow globe like it was making a hundred birthday wishes and a blizzard erupted. Aaron ran frantically around the zebra walls slowly turning into a human icicle. His nostrils burned to the scent of an earthy, mildly sweet, mint flavor and he gasped as snow covered his eyes. Passing elves, snowmen and Christmas trees, he continued to shiver and thought it'd be best to just fall over and surrender to hypothermia. The face brought a cup of hot chocolate to its mouth and took a large satisfying drink. Now practically a human glacier, Aaron groaned and crawled a few more feet. Finally, at last, he reached the EXIT sign in the maze. The sign was covered in several inches of snow and he started to dig. He dug for thirty seconds, until he saw an octagon drenched in blood. Snowflakes started to slowly sprinkle on top of the red octagon and it spelled out STOP. He looked up at the face holding the snow globe and it was Rebecca Lynn Swanson. He screamed in bloody horror and woke up with the other four boys' faces over him. Bruce was chewing his mint tobacco and a tiny piece had fallen on Aaron's shirt. A huge lightning bolt struck the backyard and it echoed within the cabin. Aaron almost flatlined and they all went back to bed without asking what he experienced while in deep REM sleep.

***

They awoke the next morning with massive hangovers. Nelson was complaining about his back being sore from sleeping on the floor. He asked Reggie to walk on top of his back to try to reduce the stiffness. Reggie did as he was requested and walked back and forth his back and pretended he was surfing. Nelson's bones cracked and he screamed uncle for Reggie to get off.

Bruce was in a rocking chair outside trying to get the hair of the dog smoking a cigar and drinking a beer. The hair of the Pitbull immediately bit back and shed all over his face, Bruce started coughing violently from the smoke and spit a loogie on the ground. He grabbed his side in pain and let out a yelp due to the gut rot and heartburn that was boiling within his body. He forced himself to go to the bathroom, which had apple cinnamon candles, perfectly wrapped towels and a picture of Travis' large family at a family reunion in the backyard of the cabin they were staying at. Sitting on the toilet, he noticed that his feet were touching the bathtub. It was certainly an inconvenience. He looked out the window and waited for the aftermath of his drinking to unleash from his body. Within seconds, he crapped violently into the toilet and vomited into the bathtub at the same time. The proximity of the bathtub and toilet had suddenly turned into a major convenience and he was now somewhat relieved as he wiped the puke off his face.

Travis made strong coffee for everyone while Aaron sat at the table writing out a grocery list to get them through the next two days. His list consisted of TUMS, eggs, cheese, onions, green peppers, blueberries, coffee, beer, bread, butter, bananas, strawberry jam, salmon and brats. The plan was for Aaron and Travis to drive to the grocery store and then cook breakfast before hashing out the final details of the pact.

Bruce yelled at everyone to come outside and see the damage sustained from the storm overnight. The beautiful eighty-foot oak tree had timbered over without the aid of a lumberjack. Mother nature clipped and clawed from the root and yanked its precious life away. The oak tree's eulogy came right after the bolt of lightning that awoke Aaron from his nightmare hours ago. The thought that Rebecca may have been aiming for the cabin spooked the living shit out of them.

"We got some work to do while they go to the store, boys," Bruce said, letting out a sigh and smacking his head to try to rid the hangover. No luck.

"Damn, even the tire swing is in pieces. I loved that thing," Travis said firmly and took a sip of his coffee.

"Come on, let's go!" Aaron patted Travis on the back.

They pulled up to Andrews' Market, which was a small Ma and Pa shop a few miles down from the cabin. Travis knew the owner very well as he had been coming to the cabin to visit his grandparents since he was a kid. The familiar wave of must and mildew of the grocery store welcomed them at the entrance.

"Trav! Wasn't expecting you and your family until the holidays," Mr. Andrews said smiling with his missing teeth. He was an older bald overweight man with thick bushy eyebrows. It looked as if two monster caterpillars were crawling across his face. He always wore jean overalls and a bird-watching hat. He loved everything about nature: the roots, bark and leaves on trees, bees pollinating flowers, the smell of cow manure roasting in the farms, photosynthesis and entomophagy. He loved snacking on fried insects. Yes, he loved everything about nature.

"Howdy Mr. Andrews, yes just stopping up to take the boat for one last cruise." Travis lied but he didn't like lying to him since he was such a good friend of his late grandfather.

"Oh? No school for you boys this week?"

"Just a few days off for teacher staffing meetings and whatnot."

"Storm scared the dickens out of me last night. My goofball cat jumped thirty feet in the air and curled on top of my face," Mr. Andrews said putting a piece of gourmet candy in his mouth. "Might as well let the caramel be the dentist for my other teeth, right?" He snickered scratching his clean-shaven face.

"Yeah, the storm took down a large oak tree last night," Travis said.

"Missy?" Mr. Andrews asked.

"Missy?" Travis said with a confused look on his face.

"That tree with the tire won it?"

"Ya?"

"We called her Missy after your great-grandmother. She planted it the day your grandparents bought the property. Once it started getting bigger, we use to carve our new year resolutions into it every year. If we didn't succeed, we'd have to scratch it off. If the task was completed, it'd stay in the tree if the Beatles liked our handwriting that is. As the years went by, more and more scratches appeared, unfortunately," Mr.

Andrews said after letting out a grunt and started to cough. He grabbed a cough drop and stared at Travis.

"Very cool, I never knew of the tradition," Aaron finally replied from the back of the store putting groceries from his list into his basket.

"Uh, huh. I'd like to come over and see it before you boys burn it," Mr. Andrews said as he rolled the cough drop around his mouth.

"Yeah, swing by over tomorrow afternoon if you'd like. We'll be gone by then. Probably will just burn the branches, but not the trunk." Travis glanced at the jar of peanut butter on the cashier counter.

"You gotta try it. Not for the taste, but for the skin. Much cheaper than shaving cream. I used some this morning. Take the rest with ya. Give it a go!" Mr. Andrews boasted with thrill about the peanut butter Travis was looking at.

"Ha-ha, okay, Mr. Andrews. I'll let you know how it goes for me." Travis picked up the jar of Justin's peanut butter. Aaron returned to the front of the store glancing at Travis. Mr. Andrews and the jar of peanut butter and let out a subtle chuckle and didn't say a word.

"You boys all set?" That'll be $30.00 even. And Aaron, here is my number if your ever in town and need a co-captain when Travis can't make it for a boys' weekend when he is being whipped around by Angela." Mr. Andrews laughed and as Aaron gave him a nod and put the number into his phone.

"Keep the change!" Travis smiled handing him two twenties. Mr. Andrews thanked him for the kind gesture and off they went.

While they were off at the store, Reggie, Bruce and Nelson walked out into the very cloudy and light drizzling day. They approached the oak tree that had fallen to the ground. There was no way they'd be able to clean up the mess while they were there, but felt it'd be best to do some kind of a chore to keep their mind off of things. They sat down on the trunk for a few moments to read some of the carvings: Find Loch Ness Monster (oddly it wasn't scratched out), Stop Biting Nails, Save A Life, Win Lottery, Write A Book, Marry Beautiful Bonnie (Travis's grandma), Lose 40 Pounds, Skinny Dip Every Summer and Stop Eating on the Shitter. After getting a small dose of laughter for some kind of sunshine to start their day, the three of them pulled large branches to the fire and started to ax them into smaller pieces.

"It's not going to burn, it's all wet," Nelson said.

"It'll burn, trust me," Bruce muttered with a chew in as he raised the ax way over his head. Nelson glared into Bruce's eyes upset that no one ever agreed with him. He swung through a large branch with an ax and connected. Chunks of wood flew up in the air and Nelson ducked.

"So, why do we have to be out here for two days anyway? Why can't we just agree to a story after breakfast and go home," Nelson said picking up small pieces of wood and throwing them on top of the fire pit.

"We gotta keep this as a base for a little bit so we can see what's going on back there," Reggie replied, cutting Bruce off, who was scratching his head becoming irritated with all of Nelson's questions.

"Well, how the hell are we supposed to do that?" Nelson asked. Bruce looked at him and shook his head ignoring him and continued to chop wood.

"Well, fuck it then. I'm going home. I don't care how much an Uber costs from here, I don't want to be here anymore. It's creepy as fuck. Plus, I didn't do shit. I didn't touch the sign. I didn't do anything." Nelson moaned and started to pull out his phone.

"Don't be fucking stupid," Bruce yelled swiping his phone to the ground. Nelson looked at him in disbelief as he dropped to his knees to pick up. Reggie snatched it off the ground before he could pick it up.

"What the fuck, you piece of shit! Give it back." Nelson pushed Reggie, but he didn't budge. Reggie shoved him as hard as he could—he fell into the firepit. If it would have been burning, Nelson would have burnt to a crisp. Reggie started to pour gasoline on Nelson's phone and threatened to light it on fire. Nelson shouted, got to his feet and ran towards Reggie with pure evil in his eyes. Nelson then speared Reggie into the ground and started wailing on him with fists. Bruce immediately pushed him off and held both of them apart as he could.

"You fucking idiot. We can't trust you. You're a fucking squealer. Tell the world everything. I almost fucking failed the 8th grade because you ratted on me for telling teachers I cheated on an exam. You really think I'm just going to let you have some random stranger pick you up where we are fucking hiding out so you can tell him everything on the drive back?" Reggie screamed as he wiped blood from his lip.

"Fucking cool it, guys. I don't want to see another body," Bruce said firmly.

"What do you mean? You saw Rebecca's body?" Nelson asked.

"No, fuck that." Bruce said shaking his head. "Nelson, why don't you grab the rest of those branches? Reggie, can you get the fire started?"

Nelson looked at Reggie holding out his hand expecting him to toss his phone back, but Reggie ignored him and started to pour gasoline in the fire pit. Nelson threw his hands up in disgust, shook his head and walked over to the branches. Reggie certainly had a reason to be concerned with Nelson's past being the gossip king. It was true that he would be higher in the ranks if he would keep his mouth shut, but Nelson thought differently. He thought that if he shared juicy gossip to others, he'd get the respect he wanted. He wanted to be a comedian so he used the incidents he witnessed to impersonate to help start his comedy career.

For Reggie it was no laughing matter. Although he was rarely a recipient of Nelson's juicy gossip, he wasn't fond of it —it almost got him in trouble. Reggie was a genius when it came to cheating on exams. Writing equations like the Pythagorean theorem on the back of his baseball hat and the notorious "sneeze (a), cough (b), grunt (c), finger snap (d)" routine. He would do this if he knew all of the answers to an exam and would do the acts to call out the answer as a password to all of his buddies in class during an exam.

One time he got really creative, very creative for an eighth-grader. He was taking a current events class he was struggling with and he would have failed it if he didn't come up with the genius idea. On exam days, he would call in sick. Later in the week, the teacher, Mrs. Pearson, would go over the exam and hand out copies of the exam. Reggie paid a kid named Danny to circle all of the answers while she reviewed the exam for the class. After the end of the exam, Mrs. Pearson would ask for everyone to return the copies. Danny wouldn't return it. He would put the exam with all the circled answers in his pocket and handed it off to Reggie who was sitting outside of the classroom. He wouldn't be allowed in the classroom during the day of the review because he was "sick."

Reggie would then have to make up the exam the next day in the library. He could obviously now ace it, but he couldn't just have a copy of the exam with the correct answers next to him while he took it. So he got a red pen and wrote the answers on his stomach one by one; not by the letters of multiple choice. Instead, he wrote it in code by letters. Triangle (A), Square (B), C (Circle) and D (Diamond). He was in the middle of taking his exam when he received a text message from

Aaron saying that Nelson had told Mrs. Pearson of his plan. Nelson was bummed he failed the exam and didn't feel it was fair for someone to get a perfect score without studying. Luckily, Reggie was spending the weekend at Aaron's place and he had shampoo and conditioner in his backpack. He squeezed a dab of shampoo on his hand and violently scrubbed the answers out of his belly. Mrs. Pearson approached him and he gladly pulled up his shirt without any red ink. He had to take the rest of the exam without the answers and barely passed. He got a D+, which was just enough to pass the class so he didn't have to retake it during summer school. During the next recess, Nelson had red ink running from his face from Reggie's pen, his fist.

Bruce took one more swing and dropped it to the ground wiping sweat from his face. The alcohol from last night was kicking Bruce's ass and he was glad to see Travis and Aaron had returned from the grocery store and drove the vehicle to the backyard. Bruce immediately walked into the cabin to get some TUMS for his agonizing heartburn. Travis was pouring more coffee and preparing the salmon for everyone. Aaron was dicing away at the onions. Travis picked up a piece of salmon and raised his other hand.

"I remember going to that same store with my grandpa and coming back with enough salmon to feed an army," Travis said. "He would always remind us of the trick to remember Alaskan Salmon. Chum is your thumb. Sockeye is your index finger. Imagine poking someone's eye out. King is your middle finger, which is also called Chinook. Silver is your ring finger or known as coho. Pink is your pinkie which is also called humpback," Travis explained as he lifted a finger calling out the mnemonic device.

Aaron set the knife down and turned to him. "Man, we don't deserve to be eating a meal like this."

"Dude, we all know it was a tragedy. But we didn't kill her, remember that. We have to get on with our lives as quickly as we can," Travis said lowering his hand and turning to season the salmon.

"The nightmare I had last night…" Aaron started to explain.

"You wouldn't believe the shit that Nelson just tried to pull." Reggie stormed into the cabin still sporting a bloody lip and holding up his phone. Nelson stood outside the door to avoid the confrontation.

"What the fuck are you talking about, Reggie?" Travis asked folding his arms and leaned against the counter. Aaron looked up and continued to chop as tears dripped down his face. Maybe they were the onions, but more than likely it was from the nightmares he experienced.

"He tried to fucking Uber out of here," Reggie yelled verifying the canceled trip.

"Nellie, what the fuck is up, man?" Travis scolded as he motioned him to come inside. Nelson didn't reply and slouched down on a recliner and started to pout.

"Quit fucking boohooing," Reggie barked.

"Would everyone just please shut the fuck up? We're not getting anywhere fighting over this shit," Aaron screamed.

"Agreed, let's talk about this in a civil manner after breakfast. Thanks for cooking, you two," Bruce said wincing as he grabbed the Tums. He popped three in his mouth and washed it down with a cup of coffee. Travis poured Bruce a glass of water from the sink, he thanked him and chugged it down in seconds.

Nelson was lowering his head and planting his hands over his face continuing to tear up. Reggie sat on the other side of the living room picking at the blood on his lips and looking at his fingernail that had blood dripping from it. Nelson was still pouting about not having his phone and Reggie tossed it at Nelson so he'd shut up. Bruce sat at the kitchen counter resting his one hand on the top of his head from the pounding headache and the other hand on his gut from the heartburn that was starting to resolve. Aaron was in the kitchen trying to reminisce about the great times he had in the cabin as a kid. It was almost as if human language became extinct—no one said a word as the breakfast was being cooked. Only agonizing moans, remorseful sobbing, the sound of onions and eggs sizzling on the stove and the birds chirping away going on with their daily lives as they darted from tree to tree. Travis became the caretaker for the group and handed Bruce some aspirin, Reggie a napkin to stop his bleeding lip, Aaron an encouraging pat on the back to say everything was going to be okay, and Nelson a cup of coffee. Travis clinked cups with Nelson and took a sip. Nelson took a big slurp.

"Wow, this is really good," Nelson said finally breaking the silence.

"Yup, my grandpa's famous morning recipe. Coffee, whiskey and a dash of cinnamon."

"Thanks, Trav."

"Don't worry, Reggie, I'm making you one too. Doesn't look like you need one now do ya, Bruce?"

Bruce tapped softly on the counter asking for one without saying a word. Breakfast was ready and Travis served the plates of eggs, toast and salmon with Irish whiskeys to everyone while Aaron started to clean up.

"We can do it after. Let's eat," Travis said.

CHAPTER 15

They all sat on the couches in the living room to eat their breakfast. Reggie flipped on the television. Bad move. The morning news was on featuring the tragic death of Rebecca Lynn Swanson. Her mother was sobbing asking the entire audience to share more details of what happened to her baby girl. It was eerily disturbing, and Reggie was just about to flip the station as scrambled eggs fell from their mouths onto their plates.

"In another shocking development, local Charlie Rivers has been found dead in his apartment. He was being questioned by police for his license plate being near the scene of the crash that took Rebecca Swanson's life early Sunday morning. A suicide note and a bottle of pills were lying next to his body. An autopsy will be conducted tomorrow morning to confirm his cause of death."

Reggie turned off the TV and looked at everyone with dread.

"Holy fucking shit! Charlie, the town drunk ran the stop sign and crashed into Rebecca's car and fled the scene?"

Reggie screamed, dropped the remote and his eyes blinked rapidly

"Well fuck, so we're responsible for two deaths now? I can't live like this." Aaron sighed as a tear dropped onto his salmon.

"Guys, guys. We still need to have an alibi in case we're ever questioned," Travis said.

"Fuck that, we gotta turn ourselves in. This is insane. I'll call my brother, he can be our lawyer," Aaron said shuffling through his pocket to receive his phone.

"Shut the fuck up, we're not calling anybody. Do you really want to throw away our futures because of a drunk driving incident that we weren't involved in?" Travis snapped back.

"We'll go to jail for this, Aaron. We can't fess up to this, dude," Bruce chimed in. Travis glanced at him and nodded his approval.

"Maybe, if we turn ourselves in, we'll just get a fine," Reggie stepped in trying to defend Aaron.

"That's a big fucking maybe. I don't want to have to take that risk. If you want to take the blame yourself, go for it. But don't you dare bring me down with it. Scholarships or even going to college goes right out the fucking window. Listen, what we did was bad, yes. But, we never intended to cause anyone's death," Travis explained and then stormed towards the door.

"Where the hell are you going?" Reggie asked trying to stop him.

"To get some fucking air. Move out of my way." Travis snapped and pushed open the screen door and walked outside and paced frantically in circles in the driveway. The rest of them sat in silence with their heads down trying to phantom how they could go on with their lives with this burning secret. Could they really take it to the grave?

"WE'RE MURDERERS!" Nelson cried dropping to the floor with his plate of food. He was having difficulty breathing due to swelling in his throat; he had a sudden drop in blood pressure, his skin was turning pale and his lips were turning blue. He started to vomit uncontrollably and Reggie, Bruce and Aaron ran to his rescue surrounding him in a circle slightly slapping at his cheeks.

"Nelson, Nelson. Wake up, what's fucking wrong?" Aaron screamed.

Bruce ran to the sink, got a glass of water and splashed it on Nelson's face. No reaction. Aaron grabbed a hold of his wrist and tried to measure his pulse. He lost count after just seconds—his pulse was beating so rapidly. He was turning more into a ghost minute by minute. He opened up his mouth and let out a horrifying hurl. Vomit projected a foot into the air and splattered back onto his face. Some of it landed on the plate of food beside him.

"Don't fucking die on me, man. Where is his EpiPen?" Bruce cried and started to sweat profusely. Aaron and Reggie stuffed their hands down into Nelson's pockets but couldn't find anything. Nelson was taken hostage so he didn't have the opportunity to pack the bare essentials, which would have included a change of clothes, toothbrush, deodorant and most importantly his EpiPen for his food allergens. Reggie inspected the plate of salmon in the pile of vomit and concluded that it caused was his allergic reaction.

"He's suffering from Anaphylaxis. We gotta call for help or else he's going to die!" Reggie screamed. Travis ran back into the house smoking a cigar and looked at them.

"Don't you fucking dare call the ambulance. That is our one-way ticket to jail." Travis took a puff from his cigar.

"What the fuck is the matter with you?" Reggie yelled and then looked back down at Nelson's almost lifeless body.

"We have to call the ambulance. This has nothing to do with our bullshit anymore. This is about saving Nelson's life. Why are you acting like such a piece of shit?" Aaron shouted and tossed his phone over to Bruce to call for help—Bruce's phone was dead. Aaron put his head down on Nelson's stomach to see if he could hear anything. Still movement, but mostly gurgles.

"Why? Why? Why? Because, I was there the night Rebecca died. So, yes, every move we make does still matter," Travis dropped a bombshell. If there would have been gasoline poured on the carpet of the cabin, the burning hot secret, the confession would have brought the entire living room up into flames.

Bruce dropped the phone from his hand and the voice of the dispatcher was in the background "Hello? Hello? Hello?"

"Oh my fucking God!" Aaron screeched in terror and stood up to face Travis expecting him to elaborate. Nelson continued to tremble in his anaphylactic shock and violently coughed up blood as he laid on his back staring into the ceiling. His face was as pale as the blizzard of snowflakes that frosted Aaron's mind during his nightmare of Rebecca. His skin began to develop a violent rash as his immune system was being attacked by the pesky proteins preventing him from getting enough oxygen. He gasped in terror and projectile vomited landing back onto his face. Behind his puke-covered face, his eyes appeared as blue as the ocean. Nelson had always dreamed of a life on the ocean. After he graduated from high school, his dream was to join his uncle's cruise company and travel back and forth to the Caribbean. He decided he'd do that for a year or two and then take hotel and tourism management courses down in Florida. His younger brother Peter would join him after he'd graduate. His blue lips weren't the color of the ocean he wanted to sail on next summer. His white pasty face and blue lips were the color of death. The color of the ocean he was sailing on had been hijacked by a red dark violent STOP sign. He was shipwrecked. Reggie, Aaron and Bruce burst into tears as a flock of birds flew outside past the window. The first greeting for Nelson's soul.

Travis didn't shed a tear and spit a huge loogie on his grandfather's carpet. Why would it matter now anyway? Coffee, eggs, salmon, blood, sweat, and vomit and tears had completely stained the carpet over the last twenty minutes. Travis took another puff from his cigar and confessed to what happened in the early morning hours of Sunday, October 15th.

"Angela and I had plans to get married right after we graduated, but I kept hearing these thoughts in my head telling me I was too young to make a commitment. After the night of Bruce's party, I started hooking up with Rebecca. We were doing it secretly for the past few months and I was beginning to fear that Angela was getting suspicious. Anyway, two nights ago, Rebecca was a little drunk and dropping me off back home when we got into a heated argument. She wanted me to break up with Angela and only see her. I told her I couldn't do that and she started smacking me in the face. I was starting to panic and buckled up just in time. Within moments, she swerved to the left to avoid the embankment and we hit it head-on. She died instantly and I crawled out of the passenger door after escaping the airbag. Her beautiful face was dismembered and just exploded blood all over the windshield. We didn't have time to stop, well… because we know why. Luckily, there was no traffic being so late in the evening so there were no witnesses. The car was totaled and I moved her over to the passenger seat. It took a few tries to start up, but I moved the car in the middle of the intersection so it looked like she didn't have a head-on collision with the embankment and another car was involved and fled the scene. I then moved Rebecca's body back to the front seat. The only scar I got was this minor cut above my left eye. Yeah, that wasn't from an infection. I fled the scene right as a semi was approaching and puked for five minutes non-stop and balled my eyes out uncontrollably. And then you know what flashed before my eyes? You guys. My best fucking friends. Our futures. Our pact to go play college football together. I felt like such a piece of shit when I moved her body back and forth. But I did it for each and every one of you because I know you'd do the same thing for me," Travis wept and pleaded for his friends to accept him.

"I hope you burn in mother fucking hell. You lied to us. You fucking lied to us!" Aaron shrieked.

Travis fell backward into the kitchen counter, and a steak knife doused in peanut butter dropped to the floor beside him. Aaron, Bruce and Reggie wiped tears from their eyes and pointed at it in disbelief. A sign of deception haunted the room.

"You killed Nelson? You fucking killed Nelson," Reggie screamed, ran towards Travis and tackled him into the refrigerator. Pictures of Travis as a younger boy holding up fish he caught on the Lake Sabathia dropped on top of him. Reggie picked up one of the photos and stared at Travis as the child and then the deranged teenager he was pinning to the ground.

"Who the fuck are you?" Reggie said breathing heavily as he held a tight grip on his wrists. Aaron and Bruce watched the battle from the living room.

"Get the fuck off me, get off me!" Travis yelled as he spit into Reggie's face. Reggie wiped the spit off and Travis punched him in the jaw. Reggie fell backward and hit his head on a cabinet. Travis frantically crawled away and Reggie grabbed at his shoe. Travis grabbed the steak knife covered in peanut butter and slashed Reggie on the left side of his face. A flap of flesh hung from his face as blood splattered across the floor. Travis got to his feet and held up the knife in his defense as Reggie dropped to his knees screaming in agonizing pain as he put both of his hands on his cut. Travis turned to Bruce who was holding a fire-stick poke and Aaron who had a lamp in his hand. Bruce grabbed for his phone.

"Drop it or I stab his fucking heart out," Travis promised gasping for air from his battle with Reggie. Bruce threw his phone to the ground. "Kick them over, NOW." Bruce kicked his and Aaron's phones over to Travis who was now standing over Reggie who was lying beside a pool of his own blood. Travis picked up Aaron's phone and smashed it against the kitchen counter into pieces. He did the same to Bruce's and then threw the damaged pieces on top of Reggie. Bruce and Aaron stepped to move closer with their weapons in hand.

"Step back or else he gets it," Travis warned. He proceeded to stick his hand into Reggie's pocket and grabbed his phone. He chucked it against the wall as hard as he could and it shattered into pieces right next to the jar of Justin's peanut butter, the poison used to kill Nelson.

"Give me Nelson's. Fucking now!"

"Why are you doing this? What the fuck is wrong with you?" Aaron cried and dropped to Nelson's lifeless body to pull out his phone. He held it in his hand for moments refusing not to pass it. Travis shook his head and stabbed into Reggie's right side of his face matching the agonizing pain on his left side.

"Just give him the fucking phone," Reggie pleaded in a hoarse voice that was no longer recognizable. Aaron tossed the phone and he caught it with one hand.

"Maybe we should have swapped football positions more often." Travis let out a demonic laugh and stabbed the phone into pieces with the knife.

"You're never going to get away with this. You fucking bastard." Bruce cried continuing to hold the fire poking stick in the air.

"It wasn't supposed to be this way, but I still planned for it. We were all supposed to survive. Well, not everyone. Nelson was going to squeal, we all know that. I didn't think he'd get poisoned that quickly. I was hoping you guys would be more understanding and trust me in my decisions. I even went over to Charlie's and tried to convince him that he was involved in a car accident. I promised him protection from the cops if he left the city and never came back. Unfortunately, he decided to have an earlier funeral. He would have probably died from liver failure in a few years anyway, so no shame there," Travis said firmly looking at Reggie's blood-soaked face. Bruce and Aaron looked at each other realizing that Travis had killed Charlie, making it look like a suicide.

The evening of the accident, Travis awoke Charlie from a drunken slumber, threatened him with a baseball bat and forced him to write the message while he was on the floor begging for his life. Travis proceeded to pull out a prescription bottle of methadone from his pocket he received from his doctor last year after a nearly fatal motorcycle accident. He opened up a bottle of whiskey on top and poured a tall pour into a very dirty glass that was in the kitchen sink. He told Charlie to say "ahh" and forced several pills and whiskey down Charlie's throat. His last meal. The last step was to frame Charlie by placing his license plate next to the scene of the crime. When Travis arrived on foot, the coroner, ambulance, fire trucks and police cars had already arrived. He overheard the police chief state they'd wait to the early mourning hours to do a more thorough investigation of the accident. Travis hid in a nearby laundromat until the coast was clear and then dropped Charlie's license plate twenty feet from the accident.

"Okay, okay, we will do whatever the fuck you want. Whatever story you want," Bruce pleaded dropping the fire stick to the ground and holding his hands in the air. Aaron peered into Bruce's eyes and dropped the lamp.

"Oh? Now, you want to listen to me?" Travis laughed madly as he held the knife in the air. Peanut butter dripped from the knife onto Reggie's face.

"Don't! Don't! Don't fucking do it!" Aaron and Bruce pleaded.

"I refuse to let my future be blessed with tragedies. I won't surrender as I am possessed with involuting my fantasies," Travis muttered. Without any hesitation, he jammed the knife into Reggie's heart and twisted it in a circle putting an end to his misery. The same knife used to stir the toxic peanut butter into Nelson's coffee was used to end Reggie's life; the dreams of scholarships, the laugher of epic future college parties and a childhood friendship that lasted nearly two decades.

Another flock of birds passed through the backyard to welcome Reggie's soul. Travis got off his lifeless body and slid backward to rest his back against the kitchen counter as he let out a roaring demonic laugh, a sound that Aaron and Bruce never heard him make before. Aaron wiped his bloody hands onto his shirt and wiped his bloody face against the sleeve of his shirt. He stared up at a sign hanging from the fireplace mantel. Be Yourself, Everyone Else Is Already Taken. Another sign of deception. He clearly wasn't himself anymore—he was now a monster. A demon. An evil spirit. He looked like a lost child abandoned at a playground. Aaron and Reggie stared into his devilish eyes and then glanced at each other realizing that Travis looked vulnerable and they had to make a decision to either fight or flight.

Aaron and Bruce started to push furniture over to Travis to barricade him inside the kitchen. Travis quickly got up from the floor and threw pots and pans back in his defense. Aaron and Bruce dodged and ducked while continuing to shove the coffee table, couches and chairs in Travis's direction. Travis was starting to get pinned up against the fridge and opened up the silverware drawer and started to throw forks, knives and spoons like they were hand grenades. Bullseye. A spoon smacked Bruce in the face. He grabbed his head wincing and a red spoon imprint shined on his forehead. Travis squeezed in his stomach to give him slightly more room against the furniture to slither like a snake down to the end of the counter. He smacked away the jar of peanut butter to the floor and reached for the steak knife set. He started to throw steak knives and one of them caught Aaron in the side of his stomach. Aaron learned forward from the sharp excruciating pain and tripped over Nelson's body. Bruce ran over, picked him up and they sprinted out the backdoor and ran to the front of the house to his truck. Aaron tripped again and struggled to get back up. He laid on his stomach fearing that within moments his body would decompose into a rotten skeleton. Bruce jerked at his shoulder, carried him up to his feet and put his arm around him like he was carrying a football and dragged him to the front yard. They could see his truck in the distance and knew this might be their only time to escape. Roadblock.

Every single tire on the truck was slashed. When Travis went outside to smoke his cigar while Nelson was choking to death on his own blood, he was also preventing anyone from leaving the graveyard he created. Two tombstones were already planted inside the cabin. Bruce noticed the keys were in the ignition of Travis' SUV and ran to the driver's seat to start the car. He ran back after Aaron who was struggling to walk with the sharp excruciating pain in his stomach. Blood seeped through his shirt down to his legs. Bruce lifted him back into the passenger seat and peeled out in reverse. Finally, a farewell to the boneyard.

"What a fucking psycho! I hope that bastard rots in fucking hell. Don't worry dude, we'll be at the hospital in no time," Bruce screamed for his life flooring down the gravel driveway toppling over a bird tree, fence and mailbox. Within seconds, Travis's SUV drove straight into a large oak tree. Blood, brain and bone bounced off Bruce's body like a billion bugs fleeing its host. Aaron looked at Bruce's gore splattered against the windshield and let out a terrorizing shriek that echoed within the isolated woodlands. There was no one in the vicinity to help. An atrocious pungent cloud of death incinerated the vehicle and Aaron gasped for air almost suffocating to death himself. He unlocked the door to escape, but was distracted from laughter behind him. Blood from Bruce's skull had ricocheted onto Travis' polo t-shirt—it was now soaking the color of a STOP sign. Travis sat in the backseat glaring the whites of his eyes with a sadistic sociopath smile showcasing a shotgun. Aaron reached for the door handle. Travis smashed Aaron in the back of the head with the gun and he whiplashed against the dashboard. A bone-chilling ache surged into the back of his head. He held his hand on his head wincing in excruciating pain, turned to the passenger seat and saw Bruce's eyes bloodshot, jaw open and blood dripping from the back of his head.

"You're damn right, I'm a fucking psycho," Travis confessed. He got out of the car and opened up the passenger side. He pulled Bruce's body out and jumped into the car which was still running. He jumped into the front seat and smacked Aaron against the head again with the gun and he went unconscious. Travis drove the SUV through the grass to the backyard and parked next to the firepit. He got out of the car and pulled Aaron out from the passenger side.

"You were my best fucking friend, my best fucking friend," Travis cried as he poured gasoline on the firewood. "It wasn't supposed to be like this, I swear. This wasn't our plan. I wanted to take you guys with me. Why did you have to fucking fight me on this? Why? Why? Why?" Travis screamed and then delivered a kick to Aaron's stomach. He let out a heavy groan, but couldn't move. Travis poured more gasoline onto the fire and the flame grew ten feet tall. He went back and carried

Nelson's body and dropped it on top of Aaron. Five minutes later, he came back with Reggie and dropped his body on top of Nelson. He had to walk back down to the end of the driveway to get Bruce. Another five minutes later, he dropped Bruce's body on top of Reggie. He looked down at the bodies and noticed that Aaron was no longer there.

"Fuckkkkkkkkkk!" Travis screamed. He kicked over the log benches by the fire pit and ran towards the house frantically searching for him. Entering the living room, he picked up furniture and flung it across the room which ricocheted off the taxidermy hanging on the walls. Blood smeared the walls and doors as he searched every room in the house for Aaron. No luck. Travis ran to his smashed-up SUV and peeled out of the driveway. In his rearview mirror, he could see the smoke from the fire rising the backyard; the same fire that he was going to use as a burial ground for his deceased friends, now enemies.

Five minutes passed and Mr. Andrews drove up to the cabin. When Bruce had previously attempted to contact the hospital from Aaron's phone, he had accidentally dialed Mr. Andrews' number, which was the most recent contact Aaron had put on his phone when he was at the grocery store earlier in the day. He stayed on the line and overheard the commotion of the boys, including the screaming pain that Reggie was enduring. At first, he thought it was all a prank. After a while, he knew it was something much more serious. It was death to his ears.

Mr. Andrews parked the car and took out his bird watching binoculars and scanned the area. Inside his lenses, he noticed blood dripping from the doorknob of the entrance of the cabin, the infuriating cloud of thick black smoke from the fire pit and a body hiding underneath "Missy," the oak tree that had fallen from the lightning strike the night before. He put the binoculars in his glove box, got out of the car and slowly crept around the backyard to examine the area. Walking past the cabin, he peeked through a window and noticed the living room floor was soaked in trails of blood and several pieces of furniture were dismantled. He cautiously walked around the side of the house tiptoeing, pulled out a knife and held it firmly in his right hand. As he reached the backyard, he let out a few coughs covering his face with a handkerchief. He noticed the body that was hiding underneath the tree was slowly moving and moaning in excruciating pain. Mr. Andrews approached the tree, put his hand on the trunk and knelt over to see Aaron grimacing and covered and soaked in bed.

"By gosh, by golly, what the hell happened to you, son?" Mr. Andrews wept looking over Aaron, who barely had any energy to keep his eyes open.

"Please... help... me... get... that... bastard..." Aaron slowly replied with tears rolling down his cheek.

"Who!? Who?!" Mr. Andrews shouted. Aaron didn't reply and his eyes shut tight. Mr. Andrews began to shake him to try to wake him for a response, but there was dead silence. He let out a moan and wept tears from his eyes with the handkerchief. He then picked up Aaron in his arms and carried him back to his car and took short breaks to recover from the smoke in the backyard. It was too hazy for him to even notice the other dead bodies lying next to the fire. Mr. Andrews opened up the door of his car and drove off down the street like a mad man with no idea of which direction to take. To the police station? To the morgue? To the hospital? To Aaron's parents' house?

CHAPTER 16

Joey was on his laptop in his basement listening to the song
Peppyrock by BTK, drinking out of a two-liter bottle of
Mountain Dew snacking on mozzarella sticks with an excel file
on his computer screen. His father occasionally gave him
projects to work on —he wanted to become a police detective.
Not only because he wanted to follow his dad's profession, but
because he wanted to eventually have the opportunity to rough
up the punk kids who were currently messing up his life. Of
course it'd be much better to use his baton, pepper spray, taser,
handcuffs and maybe even gun on his current classmates. In
addition to going on police ride alongs with his father, he
would often lock himself in the basement to read police
training manuals and watch *World's Wildest Police Videos,
Forensic Files* and *Cops* until two in the morning on school
nights.

Sitting at his desk, he glanced down at his khaki shorts and
noticed a huge grass stain on the right side of his knee. He
shook his head in disgust remembering the seniors that tackled
him and put him in an atomic wedgie while walking home
from school last week. He was then dragged on the grass as the
seniors tried to tie him up to a street sign. Luckily, his dorky

friend, his only friend Kathy came running off a school bus and started swinging her purse at the seniors as they ran away. The grass stain had been on his pants for a few days—he often wore the same pair for an entire week. His parents taught him how to do his own laundry, but cleanliness was never a priority. Studying was far more important to him because he wanted revenge so badly.

His father had assigned him to scan through a document to track all the street signs in the city to ensure they were still at their location using the RFD technology. Many of them had been stolen by several people over the last few months so they had no record of those. They were all replaced with new ones after the "Be Real, Don't Steal" initiative was put in place. The police department had spent several thousands of dollars on the equipment, but could not afford a notification system to alert them if a sign was in fact stolen. Instead, it had to be done manually and Joey was volunteered with completing that task. He sometimes filtered by the most recent signs installed with the RFD and didn't bother to check older ones that had been stolen and replaced; he didn't suspect a sign to be stolen from the same location twice.

He let out a yawn and took another sip of his Mountain Dew and some mozzarella sauce dripped on his pants right on top of the grass stain. The stain turned into a light brown with the addition of the sauce. His Chocolate Lab woke up from a nap, came over and started licking it off the pants. The dog put his nose in Joey's pocket and something dropped down to the floor. Joey turned around in his computer chair and picked it up. *An old mangled beer coaster, that he picked up in the school parking lot the day the news broke that Rebecca had passed?*

He took off his glasses, squinted, cleaned them breathing on the lenses and wiped them with his Scooby-Doo shirt that most likely hadn't been washed in over a few weeks. He put his glasses back on, looked at the coaster and noticed that street signs were sketched in a blueprint of what looked to be a party house. *Odd*, he thought. He didn't suspect anything to come of it, but he decided to filter all the nine sign categories: Dead End, Deer Crossing, 55 MPH, Railroad Crossing, Yield, Do Not Enter, No Parking, Road Work Ahead and Reserved Parking. Of course, he had to check more than nine signs, he had to check every sign that fit that description in the database. He spent over an hour scanning through the document with no luck and decided to finish it tomorrow after school. He stretched, turned to his clock and noticed it was 1:55 AM and let out a huge lawn. *Hmmmm, maybe just for the hell of it!* He did the 55 MPH—it resembled the current time. He went through all the signs one by one and his jaw dropped. He had found a match of a missing sign that was not in its current location. He typed in the address of where it was taken and then noticed where the sign was currently located. How far could have the 55 MPH sign sailed down the creek where Nelson dropped it yesterday?

***

"Pack your bags! We gotta get out of here!" Travis whispered climbing through Angela's window and waking her up.

"Oh my god! What the hell happened to you? Are you okay?" Angela yelled turning to the window as she looked at Travis' face and a shirt that was covered in blood and dirt. Her bedroom door immediately swung open to her parents worried sick.

"What happened? What happened?" Angela's father screamed as her mother looked around the bedroom for an intruder. Travis had fallen from the tree to ensure he wasn't seen and badly sprained his right leg. He crawled over to the bushes and hid.

"It was just a nightmare! I'm okay, I'm okay!" Angela hushed back to her parents. Her mother gave her a kiss on the forehead and her father went to the window and looked down and saw a few branches on the ground.

"I didn't hear any storm, but it looked like it left a little mess in the front yard," her father said. "Okay, glad you're okay. Sweet dreams, honey."

"Good night, Mom and Dad." The door shut and Angela ran to the window and peeked down.

"Travis? Travis? Where are you? Why aren't you at the cabin with the others?" Angela whispered.

"We gotta get the fuck out of here! They are after both of us! Hurry, pack your bags. We gotta get out of here right now," Travis whispered back crawling from underneath the branches.

"Who? Who is after us? What the fuck happened to you?" Angela demanded an answer.

"Aaron and Travis tried to kill me. Just grab some stuff and I'll tell you everything. We will call your parents once we are somewhere safe." Travis winced in pain from his right leg sprain.

"Okay, okay, I'm coming down now." Angela grabbed a few things and put some items in a backpack. She climbed down the window and helped Travis to the SUV as he limped.

She started to sob thinking that her life was in jeopardy and kissed Travis' bloody right cheek.

"Bruce, Nelson… they are both dead. I knew Aaron and Reggie were the ones that stole the signs the whole time, but I was too scared to rat on them because it would jeopardize their lives. I told Bruce and Nelson because I needed to tell someone. I just really needed to tell someone. Bruce and Nelson confronted them at the cabin and Aaron and Reggie killed them instantly. Then they attacked me and tried to shoot me, but I escaped through the woods, then ran back after they went to sleep and got in my car and drove her because they threatened to kill you when I was running away. Baby, I was so scared that they may have already gotten you." Travis cried weeping false tears. Angela hugged him and kissed him again on the cheek and wept herself.

"Oh my God! Oh my God! I can't believe this is happening." Angela sobbed in terror. Travis started the ignition, turned and gave her a big kiss on the lips.

"Everything will be okay." Travis was consoling her by rubbing her thigh. It was now three in the morning; he pulled out of the driveway and told her that they'd hide out at his aunt and uncle's house in Sarasota, Florida until everything was squared away with Aaron and Reggie locked up for life.

As they were nearing the exit of the city, Travis turned around and noticed he was being followed by a Jeep Cherokee. He kept taking turns to see if the car would continue to follow him. It did. He thought to himself, *there is no way it's Aaron.* He was supposedly dead and they didn't know anyone that owned a Jeep Cherokee. He finally laughed and decided it was probably just another high-school teenager having fun with a prank this late in the evening.

Eventually, he neared the intersection where the chaos initially began. He looked out the window and the newly installed STOP sign hissed back at him. Clearing his throat and blinking his eyes, the memorial of Rebecca Lynn Swanson cried out to him. Goosebumps flared up his arms and he began to profusely sweat. Angela was wrapped up in a blanket resting her head on the window. Travis looked over at her and then looked into the rearview mirror and knew something was terribly wrong. The Jeep Cherokee had led him to this intersection. He finally decided to put his car in park and approach the person who was preventing him from escaping to Florida. The Jeep Cherokee flashed its high beams on Travis, who returned the gesture of flipping the bird. The Jeep Cherokee then let out a loud horn that lasted fifteen seconds, and Travis ran to his car to pull out the shotgun he previously used on Bruce.

He pointed the gun and aimed at the Jeep Cherokee. Angela screamed out the window yelling for Travis to get back in the car. She feared it was either Aaron or Reggie driving the car, and that if they didn't try to drive away, they'd both be killed for knowing what she thought was the burning secret. Travis turned back at her and motioned her to quiet down and put her head down so she couldn't be seen, and he put the aim back on the Jeep. The driver then suddenly turned off the lights. Travis fired a bullet that smashed the windshield and within moments sirens were coming in every direction. Seven police cars barricaded Travis within the perimeter of the fatal intersection. He tried to get back in the car, but Angela locked the doors on him now suspecting he too was involved in the heinous crime. She climbed over into the trunk to try to cover herself from being hurt by any potential gunfire. As she laid down, she noticed a 55 MPH sign. The same 55 MPH sign that Nelson supposedly discarded in the creek yesterday. Apparently, he was too scared to do it and figured if he didn't get rid of it, he would be free from the crimes if he ratted on his friends once he got his opportunity. Instead, Joey got his chance of revenge by finding the bar coaster that Travis doodled on in the school parking lot and tracking down the 55 MPH sign in his vehicle. It wasn't a reflector after all; it was a sign that had an RFD chip implanted on the back of the sign.

He was now in the driver seat of the Jeep Cherokee behind him.

"Drop your gun and put your hands up right now!" One of the officers yelled from behind a squad car. Travis slammed on the window begging for Angela to open the door for him, but she didn't. She bawled her eyes out and kept her head hidden.

"Angela, please fucking open up! This is a mistake! You have to believe me!" Travis begged continuing to pound on the door. He then looked at the police officers who gave him a final warning to drop his weapon. Travis lowered his shotgun and knelt down, but then quickly got back up and fired a bullet in the cop's direction. It busted another windshield. Moments later, several rounds of ammunition were fired at Travis. His body violently wailed backyards into the STOP sign and he instantly died from suicide by cop. His frozen dead eyes locked into Rebecca Swanson's memorial staring into his eyes.

For his heroic actions, Joey was given the key to the city of Cedar Creek, an honorary badge from the police department and was allowed to keep the 55 MPH sign as a souvenir for his first cracked case. The blueprint that Travis drew up at The Lucid Owl was now being followed by Joey. He hung the sign over his bed and smiled staring before drifting away; it acted as a dreamcatcher because he began to have beautiful, vibrant, colorful dreams every night.

***

Aaron survived with the aid of Mr. Andrews. Mr. Andrews was able to cross off one of his resolutions of "Saving A Life" he had embarked on "Missy" the large oak tree in the backyard of the cabin before it was burned. Aaron was charged for manslaughter and given five-year probation since he couldn't be charged as an adult. He was also suspended from the football team and expelled from school for the rest of the school year. No more chances of finding the "Pot of Gold" that Coach Edwards always was confident that Aaron would find.

Weeks after the trial, he wanted to commit suicide but decided that it wouldn't give him the opportunity to salvage his guilt of being involved in six deaths. His therapist encouraged him to journal daily to aid in relieving his deep depression and help release the guilt. One lightly snowy November morning, he walked down to Cedar Creek and rested his back against a red cedar tree and got out his pen and notebook from his backpack.

Perhaps, I am in a state right now that I don't know how to break; this awful dread. Every morning, every night I cry until I've bled and wish that I were dead. These painful, recurring thoughts of guilt and shame won't leave my head. No matter the circumstances, friendships will last forever I've always said. Please accept my sincere apologies so I can put this tragedy, this nightmare, this suffering to bed. The healing will be a process and I acknowledge that with these tears that I have shed. For those that see this passage, I'm simply begging for my forgiveness is what you'd read.

Aaron put his pen and notebook into his backpack and he continued to rest against the tree watching the sunset arrive wondering how it was virtually impossible for no two snowflakes to be alike. Suddenly, a roaring, hollowing wind arrived and his hair flew back and he tugged onto the tree. Aaron started to have a piercing, throbbing headache that turned his cranium into a jigsaw puzzle to hell. The pain went up a notch with a violent episode of burning and itching throughout his entire body as if he was being attacked by red army ants. He got on his hands and knees and was met with paralyzing nausea.

He pleaded for this crippling hold of despair to dissipate and muttered "STOP, STOP, STOP" and groped the tree to surrender. Immediately, he hurled up vomit and was relieved of his symptoms. He hugged and rocked himself back and forth in comfort and used the back of his sweating, tremoring hand to clean his face. Perhaps, it was the evil spirits' way of telling him to leave the burial ground or a therapeutic emotional release from writing his journal entry.

Aaron turned around to face the red cedar tree and decided to replicate what Mr. Andrews and Travis' family did as a tradition by carving goals into "Missy," the deceased oak tree up by the cabin at Lake Sabathia. Aaron decided to name the tree "Donna," after his mom for all the trouble he had put her through recently. He carved "Triple-A," his initials Aaron Atwood Avery and a few goals into the tree. On his way back home, he crossed over Dunwoody & Damascus, the intersection where Rebecca was killed. He pulled the Komodor stuffed animal he won at the festival and dropped it at her memorial and wept looking at the November Beaver Moon.

***

Over winter break, he reached out to Joey and offered to train him in strength and conditioning. Joey gladly accepted and Aaron followed the same ritual that Tyler, his older brother taught him a few years back: daily lifting at the gym, running up and down the one hundred stairs at the local library every morning (even in the dead of winter) complimented with a disgusting protein shake. Towards the end of the school year,

Joey was jacked and as a freshman was named Prom King along with his new girlfriend, Angela, who won Prom Queen.

During the next spring, Aaron took online credits to obtain his GED. To make amends with Mrs. Gleason, he helped her with environmental initiatives on weekends by planting trees, cleaning up litter and educating the community on recycling benefits. To commit to the pact he had made with Reggie and Travis if they didn't go to college together, he demolished the treehouse. He donated some of the lumber to a homeless community and decided to use some of the remaining scraps for a project. Wearing a pair of Reggie's shoes and using craftsmanship skills he learned from Travis, he built a bench and painted "Best Coach Ever," "Good Luck" and "Go Silver Eagles" and "2017 State Champions." He showed up at a festival where Coach Edwards was working as a carnie and surprised him with the gift. He sobbed until his face paint came off and gave Aaron a big hug. Coach Edwards decided to have the bench installed on the sidelines of the football field. That very season, Coach Edwards finally found his pot of gold and won the 2017 State Championship, just like it said carved into the bench.

The End

ACKNOWLEDGMENTS

My first novel could not have been published without the dedication and passion that the folks at The Paper House provided me every step of the way. I'd like to thank Amy Bennett for spending months fine-tuning my manuscript into a more compelling story, Mo Raad for designing the front and back covers, Steven Kelly for creating my author's website, Jeffrey Garcia for bringing my novel to life with the book trailer, Lisa Patrick for formatting the book, and Tiffany Sears for leading the overall project to its success.

I'd like to pass the praise to Shelby Marie Studios for designing my author logo that is displayed on the back cover.

And finally, I'd like to thank my good friend, Kyle Trueblood, for spending a Saturday afternoon snapping photos of me in his studio to use for my author bio while we drank delicious cups of Joe from Milwaukee's finest, Anodyne Coffee Roasting Co.

ABOUT THE AUTHOR

Matthew J. Anderson, 'born and bred' a Cheesehead, grew up in Cottage Grove, a small town east of Madison, WI. His passion for writing started at seven years old, when one of his aunts gifted him with a shiny ballpoint pen in a pristine case on Christmas Day. He started Signs of Deception, his first manuscript when he was eighteen. Sixteen years later, at the age of thirty-four, he finally gained the courage to show it to the world and finished the remaining chapters. In his free time, Matt enjoys traveling the world, reading psychological thrillers, exploring new trails either biking or hiking, shooting hoops and rooting for all the Badger State sports teams.

CPSIA information can be obtained
at www.ICGtesting.com
Printed in the USA
LVHW081628171121
703608LV00013B/513